The Scarlet Berries of the Snow

Sheila K. McCullagh

Nelson

The Towers
of the Snow People
Hornwollen's
Island
Sheep
Pastures
The Wide River

The Country of the People of the Snow
South
erry Fields
N
W
E
S
Seal Island

When Nicholas's great-uncle Jeremy was lost at sea, he left Nicholas a picture. It was a picture of a great ring of silver, against a black background. There was a picture inside the silver ring, too. Most of the time, it was just the sea and the sky. But sometimes the picture changed and Nicholas found himself looking right through the ring, into another country.

In some strange way, when the ring glowed like silver fire it grew very large, and Nicholas found himself moving right through it, into the country in the centre of the ring.

Sometimes, he found himself on a ship; sometimes on dry land. But wherever he was, he found himself among the buccaneers of Ramir, who had become his friends.

This is another of Nicholas's adventures.

Chapter 1
The Snow Goose

It was the middle of the night. Nicholas lay in bed in his attic bedroom, fast asleep.

The room was very dark.

Nicholas had pulled back the curtains before he got into bed, but the sky outside was heavy with dark clouds. No stars were shining.

A little mouse looked out of a hole by the door of the room. Nicholas had eaten a biscuit before going to sleep, and there were crumbs on the mat by his bed. The mouse's nose twitched. She ran out into the room, and found the crumbs.

The room began to grow lighter. The silver ring, in the picture hanging on the wall opposite Nicholas's bed, was beginning to glow.

The light grew brighter still. The mouse's eyes gleamed. She looked up, startled.

Nicholas turned over in bed and the little mouse ran back to her hole.

Nicholas opened his eyes. He had been dreaming about the sea, and for a moment he couldn't remember where he was.

Then he saw the picture of the ring.

He leapt out of bed, and ran across to it. The ring was glowing like silver fire. As he watched, it grew larger and larger. Silver flames shot out into the room.

Nicholas put up a hand to shield his eyes,

and took a step forwards. The ground swayed under his feet. He shut his eyes, and took another step. The light faded. He dropped his hand to his side, and opened his eyes again.

The silver flames had died away. The night was all around him, and he was standing on the deck of a sailing ship. The sea was dark, and the waves were capped with white, but the sky was clear, and the stars were shining. There were strange curtains of white fire hanging in the sky ahead of the ship. Nicholas stood still, staring at them. They were very beautiful, and he had never seen anything like them before.

As he watched, a finger of green fire stretched up into the sky.

A cold wind swept across the deck. Nicholas shivered. He was dressed in the light shirt and trousers which he wore in Ramir, and they were much too thin to keep out the wind.

The wind was sweeping across the sea, filling the sails of the ship over his head, and making the rigging creak. It was a very cold wind, and it chilled him as he stood there, shivering.

He looked quickly about him. He didn't recognise the ship, but the door of the great cabin was only a few metres away. He went across to it, and pulled it open.

Inside, he saw a table, with chairs around it. A lighted lantern swung from a hook in the ceiling, but there was no one there.

Nicholas went into the cabin, and shut the door behind him. He was glad to get out of the wind, but he was still cold.

There were windows at the back of the cabin, with a long wooden seat under them, and there were two more doors, one on each side. He was just wondering which he should try, when the door on his right opened, and a man came into the cabin. It was Captain Harken.

Captain Harken stopped for a moment when he saw Nicholas. Then he laughed.

"So it's you, Nicholas!" he said. "I thought I heard someone. Have you just come?"

Nicholas nodded. "Yes," he said. "I found myself on the deck, and it was so cold that I came in here. Where are we?"

"Sailing north, towards the ice," said Captain Harken. "But you won't be sailing anywhere, if you stay in those clothes. I've a spare blanket in my cabin. I'll get it, and we'll make a bed for you on the long seat until morning. Then Halek will find you some proper clothing. Wait here a moment."

He went back through the door, and returned with a thick woollen blanket and a pillow.

"Here," he said, tossing them on to the seat under the windows. "Wrap yourself up in that. We'll find some warm clothes for you as soon as it's light."

"Where are we going?" asked Nicholas.

“North,” said Captain Harken. “Into the cold. We’re sailing north looking for the scarlet berries of the snow, which grow in the far north — so they say. There’s great illness in Ramir, Nicholas, and only the snow-berries seem able to cure it.

“The snow-berries come from the north. A trader brought some to Ramir, but he didn’t know where they grew or who gathers them — he bought them from another man, who sold them to him and then travelled on, into the mountains.

“We need a supply of berries for Ramir, and we’ve been sent to find a way to the north, to see if we can buy the berries from the people who live there — if anyone lives there. Or we might find the berries for ourselves, of course. But perhaps that’s not very likely.

“You’ll learn all about it in the morning. You’d better get some sleep now, and so had I. I’ll see you in five or six hours time, Nicholas, when Cass will bring in breakfast. He’ll be surprised to see you. Don’t startle him if you can help it, or he’ll drop the stew. Barnabas is in the other cabin. Downalong Joe and Halek are both sailing with us, and so is Tom Gold. You remember Tom Gold? He was with us when we sailed to the Island of Fire.”

“Of course I remember him,” said Nicholas. “I think about you all, when I’m away.”

Captain Harken smiled.

"Well, now you're among your friends again," he said. "They'll all be glad to see you in the morning. But I'll say 'Goodnight' now. Sleep well."

"Goodnight," said Nicholas.

Captain Harken went back into the port cabin, and shut the door.

Nicholas picked up the blanket, and wrapped it around him. He kicked off his shoes, and settled down on the long seat under the windows. It felt a bit hard, but he didn't mind. He was back in Ramir! He felt too excited to go back to sleep straight away, and he lay there, thinking.

Captain Harken had greeted him as if he had expected him. Nicholas had been to Ramir so often now, that Captain Harken never seemed surprised to see him. Nicholas was glad. It made him feel that he belonged in Ramir, even though he came from another country — and another world.

He wriggled down into the blanket. Perhaps he could go to sleep again, after all. The lift of the ship under him often rocked him to sleep. Nicholas gave a little sigh of great happiness, and closed his eyes.

* * *

He opened them again as the cabin door swung back with a clatter, and a buccaneer came in, carrying a big, steaming jug. Nicholas knew him. It was Cass.

Nicholas waited until Cass had put the jug safely on the table, and then he sat up.

"Hallo," he said.

Cass started, and stood there staring at him. Captain Harken might take Nicholas's coming calmly, but Cass looked as if he'd seen a ghost.

"What? Who?" he cried.

"It's me, Nick. I've come back," said Nicholas.

"Nick!" cried Cass. "But where did you come from? Does Captain Harken know?"

"I saw Captain Harken last night," said Nicholas. "He gave me the blanket. Is Halek about? Captain Harken said that he'd give me some warm clothes."

Cass drew in a deep breath, and slowly let it out again.

"I'll tell Halek," he said. "But you should give us a bit of warning, Nick! I'll never get used to the way you come and go. You're sure you're not a ghost?"

Nicholas laughed.

"You watch me eat that stew!" he said. "You'll soon see that I'm not a ghost."

The door of the port cabin opened, and Captain Harken came out. He looked at Cass, and laughed.

"You're as white as a ghost yourself, Cass," he said. "It's only Nicholas. You have to get used to him turning up from nowhere, when you sail with me."

"I'll never get used to it," said Cass.

"Well, slip off and bring him some warm clothes, anyway," said Captain Harken. "We don't want him freezing to death. Halek will find him some."

Cass disappeared without another word.

Captain Harken sat down at the table, and picked up one of the wooden bowls that were lying on it.

"Here you are, Nicholas," he said, as he filled the bowl and held it out. "Hot fish stew will keep out the cold for a bit, until you can get into some warmer clothes."

"Thank you," said Nicholas, taking the bowl, and sitting down at the table. Captain Harken helped himself to some fish stew and a hunk of bread, and began to eat.

Nicholas had scarcely had time for more than a few spoonsful of stew, when the door opened, and Halek came in, with his arms full of clothes.

"Here you are, Nick!" he cried cheerfully. "I put in some extra ones this time, before we left Ramir. I thought you might turn up. They're my brother's. Mine are a bit big for you, but I think these will fit."

"Shut that door, Halek," said Captain Harken. "The cold cuts like a knife."

Halek put the clothes down, and shut the door.

"I'm glad to see you, Nick," he said.

Captain Harken finished his stew, and pushed back his chair.

"You'd better sit down and tell Nicholas what is happening, Halek," he said. "I'm going on deck. You'll sleep in the starboard cabin, with Barnabas Brandy, Nicholas. We haven't as much room on this ship, as we have on *The Silver Dolphin.* Halek, make up a bed for him in there. Get your clothes in there, Nicholas, and tidy up this cabin, as soon as Barnabas has had breakfast."

Captain Harken went on deck, and Halek sat down at the table.

"How are you, Nick?" he asked.

"Cold," said Nicholas with a laugh. "But I'll be all right now. Thanks for the clothes."

The door of the starboard cabin opened, and a big buccaneer, with broad shoulders, red hair and a red beard, came out. It was Barnabas Brandy.

"Nick!" he cried, cheerfully. "We thought you'd be coming! You always turn up, when there's a job to be done. When did you get here?"

He pulled back a chair, sat down at the table, and helped himself to some fish stew and a hunk of bread.

"Last night," said Nicholas. "I think it must have been about midnight. Captain Harken was still up."

Barnabas nodded. "That's the time you usually drop in," he said, with his mouth full of bread and stew.

"Captain Harken said that Nick is to sleep in your cabin, Barnabas," said Halek.

"Well then, nip down and get another donkey's breakfast and some more blankets, and make up his bed," said Barnabas.

Halek got up and went out, grinning to himself.

"Well, Nick, how are you?" asked Barnabas, picking up another thick slice of dark bread and dipping it in his stew.

"Fine," said Nicholas. He did feel fine. Barnabas always made him feel at home. Even the words he used made Nicholas feel he belonged on the ship. There had been a time when he didn't know what a donkey's breakfast was, but he knew now. It was a sack filled with straw, and he had slept on one whenever he'd sailed with the buccaneers. No one ever talked about donkeys' breakfasts in the ordinary world.

"What ship is this?" he asked. "Captain Harken said we were going north, to find snow-berries. Where are we?"

"Sailing north, as Captain Harken said," said Barnabas, helping himself to still more stew. "I can't tell you much more than that, Nick, because no ship from Ramir has ever sailed up here before. But here we are, sailing north into snow and ice, and we have to make the best of it.

"This ship is called *The Snow Goose.* She was fitted out for this voyage in Ramir. She's built to stand the ice — and I hope she does, or we're in for a cold time of it! They strengthened her beams and her sides with the best oak that grows in Ramir.

"We're going right up into the north, and we don't even know how far we can sail, or what we shall find when we get there."

"The snow-berries must be very important," said Nicholas.

"They are," said Barnabas. "You can be sure of that. The scarlet berries of the snow, they call them. We've only seen them dried in Ramir, but we've got a drawing of one, so we should recognise it, if we find it."

"Who made the drawing?" asked Nicholas.

"Not Barka," said Barnabas. "Barka was the man who sold the dried berries in Ramir. He'd got the berries from a traveller — a wanderer, one of those strange folk who travel to the farthest corners of the earth, a man called Hornwollen. He'd got the drawing of the plant from Hornwollen, too — or so he said. He said that he'd met Hornwollen some years ago, and bought the berries from him.

"I've heard stories of Hornwollen, since I was a boy. There are all kinds of tales about him, so perhaps Barka was telling the truth — and perhaps not.

"Anyway, the berries worked like magic. We've had a terrible sickness in Ramir — hundreds of people died of it. But then we found that a drink made from those berries could cure the sickness.

"Barka demanded a lot of gold for the berries, but the gold didn't do him much good. He spent it on rum. He drank too much rum one night, and fell into the sea, and that was the end of him. We found his body the next day, washed up on a beach.

"No one knew where Hornwollen was. He hasn't been seen in Ramir for years. So the Council of Ramir decided to fit out a ship, and send Captain Harken north, to see if he could find the scarlet berries. They chose Captain Harken, because he's the only captain in Ramir who has sailed a ship in a sea full of ice — except Martin Quinn, of course, but he was away in the south.

"Barka said the berries came from a land which was as far north as a ship could sail, up beyond The Strange Land. He talked about ice and snow. He said that it was so cold there, that the sea itself froze.

"We don't know whether he was right. He only knew what Hornwollen told him — or what he *said* Hornwollen told him. I didn't trust Barka, myself.

"It's not much to go on, but it's all we have. The people of Ramir need those berries.

"Captain Harken chose this ship for the journey. She's broader in the beam than our own ship, *The Silver Dolphin,* and she can sail in closer to the shore. They made the hull of the ship stronger, with extra planks and beams.

"Captain Harken called the ship *The Snow Goose*. He'd seen the white snow geese flying north in the spring.

"So here we are, and now you know as much as I do."

The door opened, and Halek came in, dragging a big sack, full of straw, and carrying a pillow and two thick blankets.

"Here you are, Nick," he said.

"Put 'em in my cabin, Halek," said Barnabas. "Wrap yourself up in those blankets, Nick, and you'll be as snug as a flea on a cat's back. They wove them specially for us in Ramir. They're very thick and warm.

"You'd better get those warm clothes on, too. It's as cold as a fish's tail outside."

Barnabas got up, and went out on to the deck. The cold air blew into the cabin, as he went through the door.

Nicholas picked up the clothes, and took them into the starboard cabin.

"There you are, Nick," said Halek, as he folded the blankets, and put them on the bed. "Sleep on one blanket and wrap the other one round you, and you'll dream that you're cooking over the fire!"

Nicholas laughed.

"I shan't mind that!" he said.

Halek had made up his bed on the floor, against the wall on one side of the cabin. There was a bunk on the other side, where Barnabas slept.

Halek left, shutting the door behind him.

Nicholas dropped the clothes on his bed, and began to put them on. They really were warm. There was a warm vest, with long sleeves, to go under a blue shirt. There were thick woollen pants, that came down to his ankles, and thick woollen socks, that came up above his knees. There were thick trousers to go over them, and a jacket and scarf to go on top. There was another long jacket with a warm, lined hood, to wear outside. There were two pairs of gloves, one pair made of woollen cloth, with fingers, and one pair of mittens made of skins, to go over the woollen ones. Halek had brought a pair of heavy, lined boots, too, to wear on deck.

Captain Harken, Barnabas and Halek had all been wearing clothes that were much the same as the ones Nicholas was putting on. He got into them quickly, and felt warm almost at once. He folded up his light clothes, and put them on a shelf over his bed.

He went back into the great cabin. Halek had gone. Nicholas folded up the blanket Captain Harken had given him. He was just wondering whether he should leave it in Captain Harken's cabin, when the door to the deck opened, and Cass came in.

"I'll tidy up in here, Nick," he said. "You go out on deck. There's a lot to see just now. There's a great island of ice floating by."

"Thanks," said Nicholas. He gave Cass the blanket and went outside.

Chapter 2
The North Arcons

Halek and half a dozen buccaneers were standing at the ship's side, gazing across the dark water.

The wind had dropped, and they were sailing slowly past a great iceberg. The iceberg was half a mile away, and it shone with a dazzling whiteness against the blue sky.

Nicholas went over to Halek.

"Do you remember the icebergs in the far south, Nick?" asked Halek, as Nicholas stood beside him, looking out to sea. "You remember the South Arcons, and the Island of Fire?"

"Yes," said Nicholas. "The icebergs were even bigger there. Do you remember the great iceberg with the cave in it, where we hid while the Arcons sailed by?"

"I remember it, all right," said Halek. "I'll never forget it. Tom Gold was sailing with us, then. He's on board now. Did you know?"

"Captain Harken told me," said Nicholas. "I'm glad."

"So am I," said Halek. "Tom Gold's a good man to have with you, if you run into trouble."

"What trouble do you think we might run into?" asked Nicholas.

"You never know, when you're sailing in a strange sea," said Halek. "Did you see those curtains of fire in the sky last night? We've seen them for three nights, now.

"And we might even run into an iceberg! Just look at that one! Think what it would be like, if we hit that. It would be worse than hitting the Headland of Dunlorn."

"It's a *fantastic* iceberg," said Nicholas, staring across the sea at the great castle of ice, with its towers sparkling in the sunshine.

"There's something not so fantastic ahead," said Halek. "Look!"

Nicholas looked forwards, the way Halek was pointing. A thick, white band of fog lay across the sea ahead of them. The sky was clear above it, and the sea was clear up to it. The fog lay across the water like a wall made of cotton wool.

"All hands on deck!" cried Barnabas Brandy. There was a clatter, as the buccaneers came up from below. "Up on the poop deck, the first seven of you. The rest get to the ship's side, and keep a good look-out. Sing out the moment you see any ice."

Nicholas went along to the bows of the ship, and stood there, watching, as they sailed nearer and nearer to the white wall of fog.

The change was a sudden one. One minute they were under a clear blue sky. The next minute, the blue of the sky misted over, and a minute later, they were in a thick, white fog. It closed around them like a blanket. They could see nothing but a patch of dark sea and a wall of white mist.

"Downalong! Get up to the crow's nest and keep watch ahead," called Captain Harken. "Shout if you see a patch of white fog — there may be another iceberg behind it."

Downalong Joe ran back from the bows of the ship, where he had been keeping watch. He climbed up the rigging to a barrel that had been slung high up on the foremast.

They sailed slowly on.

There was very little wind, but the fog was cold. Captain Harken kept just enough sail on the ship to keep her moving gently through the water.

It seemed to Nicholas that they were moving in a dream. All he could see was the ship, and a few metres of sea around her. Every buccaneer was on his toes, ready to act quickly if there was a cry of 'Iceberg' from the crow's nest, or the ship's side. But nothing happened. They sailed on and on, in the thick white fog.

Nicholas lost all sense of time. They seemed to have been in the fog for hours.

Then, as suddenly as they had entered it, the thick white blanket which hid the sea and the sky all around them thinned to a faint mist, and the next minute they were out of the fog, and sailing under a blue sky again.

Nicholas looked out over the waves. The white wall of fog lay across the sea behind them, but ahead of them, and on each side, the sky and the sea were clear and blue again. There were no icebergs. Three or four sea-birds flew towards them, and circled around the ship.

"Land ho!" cried Downalong Joe from the crow's nest. "Land on the port bow!"

"Land it is!" called Captain Harken. "Bring up the spy-glass from my cabin, Alwar!"

Nicholas stared over the sea, the way Downalong Joe was pointing. He could see a dark line, like a cloud, lying on the water.

One of the buccaneers went into the great cabin, and came back a minute later with a telescope, which he took up to Captain Harken on the poop deck.

Nicholas ran up on to the poop deck behind him. He could see more from up there, and Captain Harken didn't seem to mind where he went on the ship.

Captain Harken took the telescope, and looked towards the land.

"Green hills," he said to Barnabas Brandy. "And — there's a ship, Barnabas. A long ship with a square sail. One of the Arcons' ships — or something very like one."

He handed the telescope to Barnabas Brandy.

"The North Arcons!" exclaimed Barnabas, looking through the telescope. "Who'd have thought they'd have sailed as far north as this! Do you think they'll fight?"

"There's no reason why they should," said Captain Harken. "We're not here to attack them, or take anything from them. We've a good ship, full of buccaneers. They couldn't hope to capture us, unless they caught us sleeping. And they won't do that!

"No, the Arcons aren't pirates. They may even be able to help us. They may know where the scarlet berries grow. The Arcons are always willing to trade — if you have enough gold to meet their prices."

"There's only one Arcon ship," said Barnabas, handing the telescope back to Captain Harken.

Captain Harken nodded. "Let's hope it's the only one," he said. He looked up at the crow's nest. "There's an Arcon ship over there, Downalong," he called. "Can you see her?"

"Just about, Captain," cried Downalong.

"Keep an eye on her," called Captain Harken. "And keep a sharp look-out for any others, too."

"Aye, aye, Captain!"

Downalong shaded his eyes with his hand.

As *The Snow Goose* sailed nearer and nearer the land, they could see that the Arcons' ship was sailing out to meet them.

They shortened the sails on *The Snow Goose.* Captain Harken sent Alwar to the bows with a long line, with a lump of lead on one end, sounding to see how deep the water was.

They could see the land clearly from the

deck now. There was a long point running northwards. They could see an opening to a bay behind it, and green hills on the far side of the bay.

The Arcons were at the ship's oars. As they came nearer, Nicholas could see a big man at the back of the ship, standing at the steering oar. He looked bigger even than Barnabas Brandy. He had thick golden hair, and a golden beard.

"Heave to!" cried Captain Harken. "They're coming over to talk to us. Can you see that flag at their masthead, Barnabas? Isn't that a flag of peace? Halek, get the peace flag from the great cabin, and run it up on the foremast!"

Nicholas could see a little blue and white forked flag, fluttering from the mast of the Arcons' ship.

Halek ran off to the great cabin and came back with the flag.

Nicholas looked upwards. There was very little wind, but the flag of Ramir floated from the mainmast, and he saw the little blue and white flag, flying out ahead of it, as Halek ran it up the foremast.

The Arcons' ship came within hailing distance. The men at the oars held her steady, on the calm, smooth sea.

"Who are you? Where do you come from, and where are you going?" cried the man at the steering oar.

"We're *The Snow Goose,* sailing from the city of Ramir, up into the far north," Captain Harken called back. "What ship are you?"

"*The Fire-bird,* from the Land of the North Arcons," the man shouted in reply. "I am called Ulf the Strong. Who are you?"

"Francis Harken, captain of *The Snow Goose.* We come in peace. We're sailing north. We should be glad if you can tell us anything of the winds and currents we shall meet."

There was some quick talk among the Arcons. Then Ulf shouted to them again.

"Do you see that little island, lying off the point? We will drop three men on that island. Send a boat with three of your men over there to join us. They shall come and go in peace."

"Drop your men, and pull *The Fire-bird* back, and we'll join you," Captain Harken called.

"They're not taking any chances, are they?" said Barnabas Brandy. "Do you think it's a trap?"

Captain Harken shook his head. "No," he said. "The Arcons are good fighters, but you can trust them, if you're friends with them. They might make us prisoners if there were only two or three of us, but they won't try and fight a whole shipload. Ulf said we could come and go in peace. I'll trust him.

"Tom Gold!"

Tom Gold ran up the steps to join Captain

Harken on the poop deck. He looked just as Nicholas remembered him, except that he was wearing thick woollen clothes, like everyone else.

"You come with me Tom, and we'll go across to that island," said Captain Harken. "I'm going to take Nicholas, too. If I take a boy, the Arcons will know that I'm not trying to trap them.

"I'll leave you the spy-glass, Barnabas. Keep an eye on us, and move across if there's any sign of trouble."

He went down on to the main deck, followed by Tom Gold and Nicholas.

Nicholas was excited at being taken to meet the Arcons. He hadn't expected it, and he was very glad to go.

Tom Gold clapped him on the shoulder as they reached the main deck.

"I heard you'd come, Nick," he said. "I'm glad to see you."

"I'm glad to be here," said Nicholas.

The Fire-bird was already at the little island. They saw three Arcons land, and then *The Fire-bird* pulled a little way out to sea again.

Captain Harken took *The Snow Goose* over towards the island, until they were about as far away from it as *The Fire-bird.*

They dropped anchor, and the buccaneers lowered the jolly boat. Captain Harken, Tom Gold and Nicholas climbed down into it.

Tom Gold rowed, and Captain Harken steered them across to a little sandy beach, where they could see the Arcons waiting for them.

Captain Harken ran the boat alongside some rocks, which they could see at one end of the beach. They climbed out, tied the boat to a rock, and made their way across the rocks to where the Arcons stood waiting.

They stopped a few metres away from them.

"Greetings," said Captain Harken quietly. "As you see, we come in peace. I have brought only a man and a boy here with me."

Ulf the Strong, who seemed to be the leader of the Arcons, nodded his head and stepped forward.

"Greetings," he said in reply. "You may come and go in peace if you wish — and if you mean no harm. Why are you here?"

"We have come to look for the scarlet berries of the snow," said Captain Harken.

Ulf's eyes widened in surprise.

"The scarlet berries of the snow? But they are only found in the far north."

"We are sailing north," said Captain Harken.

"Why are you searching for the berries?" asked Ulf.

"There is sickness in Ramir. Only a drink made from the berries will cure it," said Captain Harken. "If you have such berries, we will buy them from you for a fair price. If not, we should be glad of anything you can tell us about where we can find them.''

Ulf looked at Captain Harken without saying anything for a moment or two. Captain Harken waited quietly.

Ulf seemed to make up his mind that there was no danger.

''If that is all you want, we will help you, if we can,'' he said. ''You are not planning to stay here? You are not looking for land, where you can live?''

Captain Harken shook his head.

''As soon as we have the berries, we shall sail south,'' he said. ''If this is your land, no one from Ramir will try to take it from you. We live in the south. There is plenty of land for us in Ramir.''

Ulf looked at him again, as if he were trying to decide whether Captain Harken was telling the truth. After a moment, he nodded his head again, as if he were satisfied that he was.

''We will share a dish of fish and salt with you, as a sign of friendship between us,'' he said.

One of the Arcons standing behind him handed Ulf a small shell, with a little cooked fish in it. He opened a small bag, and took out some salt, which he sprinkled on the fish. Nicholas saw that Ulf was careful to move slowly, so that everyone could see what he was doing.

Ulf took half the fish himself, and handed the other half to Captain Harken.

"Let this be a sign of friendship between us," he said.

"May our friendship last until the end of time," replied Captain Harken.

Nicholas thought that Ulf and Captain Harken sounded almost as if they were chanting a spell.

Ulf the Strong smiled. It was clear that Captain Harken had said the right words.

"Now we can trust each other," he said. "We live here, in this land. Our houses are on the shores of the bay, in behind the point.

"Bring your ship into the bay, and anchor there. Come ashore with as many men as you like. We will hold a feast tonight. It's not often that we have visitors!

"There are men among us who have sailed north, and they can tell you about the currents, and the wind that comes down from the north, bringing the ice with it, at the end of the summer.

"We can tell you about Hornwollen, the traveller, too — and about the People of the Snow."

"That is just what we need to know," said Captain Harken. "We'll anchor, and come ashore, as you say."

"Then we will go and make the feast ready," said Ulf.

He turned and waved to the Arcons' ship. It began to move in towards the island, to pick them up.

Captain Harken, Tom Gold and Nicholas made their way back across the sands to the rocks. They climbed into the boat, and Tom Gold rowed them back to *The Snow Goose.*

Chapter 3
The feast

"Do you think these Arcons are to be trusted?" asked Downalong Joe, as he sat at the table in the great cabin, with Captain Harken, Barnabas Brandy, and Tom Gold.

(Nicholas was sitting quietly on the long seat in the window, listening.)

"I'm sure they are," said Captain Harken. "I've had dealings with the Arcons before. If they eat fish and salt with you, as a sign of friendship, then you're friends with them for life. *The Snow Goose* and its crew are safe from these Arcons — not from others, perhaps, but from the ones who live with Ulf the Strong.

"I'll take Barnabas across to the feast tonight and leave you in charge of the ship, Tom. And I'll take ten of the ship's company, too. We mustn't take too many. It wouldn't be fair to the Arcons. We don't know how many of them there are. We've only seen one ship, so I don't think there can be very many. And we don't know how much food they have. It's summer now, but the winter must be bitterly cold, here in the north — colder than we can imagine. They'll give us a feast, because that's a sign of friendship. But we mustn't eat too much of their food.

"These Arcons have met Hornwollen — or at least, they have news of him. It was Hornwollen who gave Barka the scarlet berries of the snow. Perhaps they can tell us where to find him. It's a great bit of luck for us, finding them here.

"I shall take presents across with me tonight, to the feast. That's something the Arcons always do. We'll take three barrels of flour. They won't be able to grow corn so far north, and they'll need flour. We'll take two barrels of wine, too, and I'll take a golden brooch from Ramir as a present for Ulf.

"See everything's loaded into the boat, Downalong. Barnabas will come with me. I'll take Nicholas, too. Taking the boy was the right thing. Ulf knew we came in peace, as soon as he saw Nicholas. Cass and Peran can row us across, and then come back for the others."

* * *

Two hours later, *The Snow Goose* rode at anchor in the bay, and Nicholas was in the boat with Captain Harken and Barnabas Brandy. The boat was loaded with barrels of flour and wine. Barnabas Brandy had added a big jar of honey, too. Peran and Cass were at the oars, as they slid through the still blue water towards the sands in the bay. Ulf the Strong was waiting for them on the shore, with the two men who had been with him on the island.

He held out his hand to Captain Harken, as he swung himself over the side of the boat, and walked up the beach.

"Welcome," he said. He turned to the

others. ''This is Rungar, and this is Karn.''

The two men stepped forward. Captain Harken greeted them. Then he turned back to Barnabas and Nicholas, and told the Arcons their names.

''Nicholas is your son?'' asked Ulf.

Captain Harken shook his head.

''No, but I wish he were,'' he said.

''Your adopted son?'' asked Ulf.

Captain Harken thought for a moment. Then he nodded. ''Yes, you could say that,'' he said. ''Yes. I have no children, and Nicholas's father is dead. When he is with me, he is my son.''

Surprise and happiness left Nicholas gasping. His face shone with delight.

Captain Harken smiled at him.

Ulf looked at Nicholas.

''In my country, we often adopt another man's son, if his father is dead,'' he said. ''You are Captain Harken's son. You are very welcome.''

''Th — thank you,'' stammered Nicholas. He was so happy that he could scarcely speak.

While they had been talking, Cass and Peran had lifted the barrels out of the boat, and set them down on the beach.

''I have brought these for you, as gifts of friendship,'' said Captain Harken. ''They are barrels of flour and wine.''

Ulf the Strong laughed. ''We did well, when we made friends with you, Francis!'' he exclaimed. ''We make a drink with berries, but we have had no real wine for two years. And we have had no flour for three. We shall have bread tonight! We had almost forgotten what bread tasted like."

"There's a big jar of honey, too," said Barnabas Brandy.

All three Arcons laughed with delight.

"It will indeed be a feast!" cried Rungar. "We'll carry your gifts up to our houses now, so that we can make bread for this evening."

Everyone helped to carry the barrels of flour and wine, and the big jar of honey, up the beach to the grass.

Nicholas saw a fence ahead of them, made of wooden poles. There was a gate in it, and as they reached it, the gate opened.

He could see many more Arcons standing on the other side of it — men, women and children.

There was a lot of excited talk, as they handed over the barrels, and the jar of honey.

Then Cass and Peran went back to the boat, to bring the other buccaneers over from the ship, and Captain Harken, Barnabas and Nicholas went with Ulf, and seven or eight Arcons.

Nicholas looked at everything around him. They were following a path made of flat stones, which ran across a wide field of short grass. There were nine or ten sheep in the field, and he could see more sheep on the far side of the wooden fence. Two goats were tethered to a post near the path.

In the middle of the patch of grass, he saw three long houses, all joined together. There were two other houses behind them. They had strong wooden door posts, and wooden doors, but the walls of the houses were made of piled turf, and green grass covered the roofs. The houses had no windows, but there was a trapdoor in each roof, rather like a skylight. The trapdoors were all open, and smoke was drifting up out of them.

Ulf led them to the biggest house, the one in the middle of the three, and they followed him inside.

The house seemed to be full of Arcons.

There was a fire in the middle of the room. It was made of logs, and the flames lit the whole house.

There was one large, long room. Nicholas could see wooden platforms on each side of it, about half a metre above the ground, and these were covered with sleeping bags made of sheepskins with the wool inside.

Arcons were sitting on the platforms. They got up as Ulf came in, and made room for the newcomers. The women were dressed in white woollen tunics, that ended above their knees. They wore thick, white leggings under them, tied with red leather thongs, which they had bound criss-cross around their legs. Their tunics had gaily coloured borders of red and blue. The floor of the house was just hard earth, and the women had thick boots, made of skins, like the men.

For a few minutes, Nicholas found it difficult to see what everything was. Not all the smoke escaped through the hole in the roof, and his eyes began to smart. But in a little while, he got more used to it.

There was a doorway at each end of the room, leading to another house. He could see the fires in the other houses through the doorways. They were crowded with black pots, and the smell of cooking drifted through.

The arrival of the barrels of flour and the wine and the honey was greeted by everyone with cries of delight. It wasn't long before the next boatload of buccaneers arrived, to add to the noise and confusion in the house.

But at last everyone settled down on the wooden platforms, with the fire in between. It was warm and comfortable, though the air was thick with smoke and the smell of the cooking.

They began to talk.

First, Ulf the Strong wanted to know everything Captain Harken could tell him about the voyage of *The Snow Goose,* and about the ship itself.

Captain Harken answered all his questions, and told him a little about Ramir and its people, before he began to ask questions himself. But as soon as he did, Ulf answered him readily. It was quite clear that, now they had eaten fish and salt together, the Arcons treated the buccaneers as their friends.

"Hornwollen has been here," said Ulf, in answer to a question from Captain Harken. "He came here five years ago, travelling north. He's a strange man. He had no ship of his own. He came here with a party of Arcons, who had sailed up to visit us, and to explore the country.

"They turned back, when we told them that there was nothing but ice and snow to the north of us. But Hornwollen left them, and went on alone, with a sledge pulled by four great dogs. He had brought them with him in the ship."

"Where was he going?" asked Captain Harken.

Ulf hesitated for a moment. Then he said slowly: "Hornwollen said that he was going to look for the People of the Snow."

As he spoke, he held up his left hand for a moment, with his first finger curled around the top of his thumb, and the other three fingers stretched out. All the other Arcons did the same thing.

"Why do you do that?" asked Barnabas Brandy.

"It is the sign against magic," said Ulf. "The People of the Snow are a magic people. They live in the ice. One moment you can see them, and the next moment they have vanished.

"Haven't you seen their lights in the sky? It is still summer now, and the sky never gets very dark, but you must have seen their curtains of fire, hanging in the sky. When the cold dark nights come in autumn, the People of the Snow light up the whole sky with their curtains. They turn the clouds red, and send fingers of green fire up into the air.

"It is the People of the Snow who have the scarlet berries you are looking for — or so Hornwollen said. He was looking for the scarlet berries himself. He said that he had met the snow people once before, and that they had given him the scarlet berries of the snow. If you have seen these berries in Ramir, he must have told the truth."

"Can you grow the berries here?" asked Captain Harken.

Ulf shook his head.

"We've never seen them," he said. "They belong to the People of the Snow. Even if we found them, we shouldn't touch them. There were some people who came here once, from a country called Alunka. They had been in the north. They said that they had been living there, but they had been driven out by the People of the Snow. They sailed south. But a storm came, and their ship was wrecked.

"We know that, because parts of the ship were washed ashore. We never saw any of the men from Alunka again."

"Have you ever seen the People of the Snow?" asked Captain Harken.

Everyone was suddenly very still.

Ulf the Strong swallowed. Then, after a moment, he nodded, and made the sign against magic.

"I saw three of them once, on the shore of a bay, when we sailed far into the north," he said slowly. "We had gone as far as a ship can go. There was nothing but ice in the sea ahead. The sea was like a field of ice, and the shore was covered with snow.

"There was a strange, wild cry, that rang through the air. We looked, and saw three men on the shore, dressed in silvery-white. They shone for a moment, as the moon shines. And then they vanished.

"We turned back, and rowed south as hard as we could. Even then, we were nearly caught in the ice. It closed all around us, and we thought we were lost. But a lane of water opened in the ice ahead of us, and we managed to make our way through.

"I have never been back, and I advise you not to go. You have a fine ship out there in the bay. But if the ice closes in on it, it will break like an eggshell. The People of the Snow do not want us in the north. It is they who send the ice down on us, to drive us back. That is what I think."

"Did Hornwollen come back?" asked Alwar, one of the buccaneers.

Ulf shook his head.

"Either he died in the cold, or else the People of the Snow caught him, and made him a prisoner," he said. "Perhaps the bears killed him. There are great white bears, who live up there in the ice. They can break a man's skull with one blow of their paws. We have not seen Hornwollen, or heard from him, since he left us."

"Perhaps he found another way out of their country," said Captain Harken.

"Perhaps," said Ulf.

There was a minute or two of silence in the house.

Then Barnabas Brandy gave a great laugh. He didn't sound very happy, and Nicholas guessed that he was trying to cheer them up.

"Well, I hope you'll see *us* again," he said. "We shall have to go, Ulf. We've been sent from Ramir to find the scarlet berries of the snow, and we'll have to try to find them — even if that means fighting bears or meeting these strange people you've been talking about."

Ulf looked from Barnabas Brandy to Captain Harken.

Captain Harken nodded.

"Barnabas is right," he said. "We're under orders from Ramir. We need the scarlet berries, to cure the sick in Ramir. We have to sail north."

Ulf shrugged his shoulders.

"I can see that you have to go," he said. "We won't go with you, but we'll do what we can to help you.

"If you are going, you should start at once. You should sail in the morning. There's a change coming in the weather. The summer is very short, and as soon as it is over, the sea will freeze.

"We shall be sorry to see you go, when you have only just come. We haven't seen another ship, since our friends came years ago. But you are now our friends, and if we are going to see you again, you must sail north as soon as you can, before the winter comes. I will tell you all I know about the winds, and the currents, and the ice that comes down from the north."

He took a stick, and began to draw a map on the earth floor.

Captain Harken and Barnabas bent over it, watching. The talk was all of currents and rocks, and fields of ice.

All the others began talking among themselves, except Alwar. Nicholas noticed that Alwar sat by himself, saying nothing. His face was rather white, and Nicholas guessed that he was feeling frightened.

Nicholas was sitting next to a boy called Hoon. Hoon began to ask him about *The Snow Goose,* and about life in Ramir.

Nicholas found it difficult to answer all his questions, so he started asking questions himself, and Hoon was soon talking about the way the Arcons lived, and the wonderful voyages they had made towards the north.

The time passed quickly, and the day ended with a great feast. They sat on the wooden platforms round the fire, and the great pots of food were taken round. There were stews, full of meat, and dishes full of fish. There was a great bowl of berries, sweetened with honey.

The Arcons had made flat cakes, rather like thick, small pancakes, from the flour. They cooked them on hot stones around the fire.

There were different kinds of cheese, made from goat's milk, and many dishes which Nicholas couldn't recognise. The buccaneers held back, and ate slowly. But the Arcons ate until they couldn't eat any more. Nicholas wondered how some of them could eat as much as they did, but he could see that, for the Arcons, sharing the feast was like signing a treaty of friendship.

When it was over, one of the Arcons brought out a small harp, and began to sing. The songs were all about the voyages of the Arcons' ships to strange lands, across strange seas, and about fighting with men and with dragons.

Nicholas thought that he would never forget the scene: the Arcons and buccaneers crowded together around the fire, with the firelight on their fierce faces. Brass brooches gleamed on their cloaks, and silver goblets, full of wine, shone in the firelight.

Captain Harken had given Ulf a golden brooch which he had brought from Ramir, and Ulf had given Captain Harken a short Arcon sword in return. The brooch and the sword both shone and sparkled, as the flames of the fire blazed up.

By the time they left to go back to the ship, Nicholas's head was spinning with the heat and noise, and he was glad to get out into the cold air.

They rowed back to *The Snow Goose* over the silent sea.

"That was a feast worth having!" exclaimed Barnabas Brandy, as Cass, Peran, Alwar and one of the other buccaneers pulled the boat away from the shore.

Captain Harken nodded.

"We've left friends behind us," he said. "You need friends, in a country like this."

He looked at Nicholas.

"How did you like the evening?" he asked.

"It was fantastic," said Nicholas.

Captain Harken laughed. "It was an evening to remember," he said.

But as Nicholas snuggled down under the blanket on his bed in Barnabas's cabin, the thing he remembered most was not the great feast in the houses of the Arcons. It was Captain Harken's words, when he said that Nicholas was his adopted son.

Chapter 4
Into the ice

"Well, Nick," said Barnabas Brandy, as they sat down to breakfast three days later. "How does it feel, to be part of Ramir? We've been so busy since we left the Arcons, I haven't had time to ask you."

"What do you mean?" asked Nicholas.

"The captain's adopted you as his son," said Barnabas. "He said so."

"Did — did Captain Harken really mean that?" asked Nicholas.

"Of course he did," said Barnabas. "Surely you know Francis Harken well enough by this time, to know that he means what he says? He said right out, in front of us all, that you were his adopted son. So you are. That's how we do it, in Ramir. Your own father's dead, isn't he?"

Nicholas nodded.

"Then, by the laws of Ramir, Captain Harken can adopt you as his son," said Barnabas. "And that's what he did the other night. I could see you were surprised, but I wasn't. I've seen it coming for a long time. How do you feel about it?"

"It makes me so happy that I can scarcely believe it," said Nicholas.

Barnabas laughed. "Well, you'd better get used to it," he said. "But don't let it go to your head! He's still the captain of the ship, and you're still the ship's boy!"

The door opened, and Tom Gold came in.

"The captain wants you on deck, Barnabas," he said. "There's a bit of ice in the sea. There's land in sight on the port bow, too."

Barnabas pushed back his chair, and went out with Tom Gold, leaving his mug of fish stew uneaten.

Nicholas swallowed the last bit of stew in his own mug, and followed them.

It was much colder. The ship was sailing north, under a grey sky. The wind was from the west, and clouds were beginning to blow up.

A long way to the west, Nicholas could see cliffs, with hills rising behind them. The cliffs looked dark and dangerous, and the hills were covered in snow. Small hummocks of ice were floating by in the grey sea.

Nicholas had expected the ice to be flat, but it wasn't. It was carved into strange shapes by the wind and the waves. He saw one piece floating towards them that looked like a sleeping lion, and another that looked like a great white bear.

Captain Harken was standing on the poop deck.

"Reef the main sail!" he cried.

Some of the buccaneers were already climbing up the rigging, and others ran to the ropes.

It was hard and dangerous work. The sail was stiff with ice, and little bits of loose ice fell down on the deck.

Captain Harken shouted more orders.

Nicholas climbed up the steps to the poop deck. The steps were slippery with ice, and he had to hold on to the rail.

"There's a storm coming, Barnabas," he heard Captain Harken say. "And there's no shelter for us under those cliffs."

"The sky is lighter ahead," said Alwar, who was standing nearby. "It almost looks as if the sun is trying to break through. See — over there, ahead of us."

"I can see it, and I don't like it," said Captain Harken. "That's not the sun, Alwar. Those clouds aren't over the dark sea. They're drifting over ice and snow. It's not sunlight that you can see ahead. It's the white of the ice, shining up on to the clouds.

"Get up into the cross-trees," he called to Peran, who was crossing the deck. "Keep a sharp look-out for icebergs."

Peran ran over to the foremast. Nicholas watched him climb up the rigging, into the barrel which was lashed to the cross-trees.

Almost at once, he shouted back to them: "There's ice ahead! It stretches right across the water, as far as I can see."

"I thought so," said Captain Harken. "We'll have to reef still more, Barnabas. Reef the top sails."

Barnabas went down to the main deck, and began shouting orders.

Captain Harken sent Nicholas down to the great cabin for his spy-glass.

When he brought the telescope back, Nicholas stayed on the poop deck, watching the buccaneers climbing the rigging. Every moment, he expected one of them to slip and fall. But they didn't, and in time all of them returned safely to the deck.

"There's hail coming," said Barnabas Brandy, looking out to sea.

"Not hail — snow!" said Captain Harken, putting the telescope away.

In a few moments, the air was full of snowflakes. The far cliffs and mountains, and the floating ice, all vanished, hidden by a curtain of falling snow.

Nicholas pulled the hood of his jacket over his head, and tied the leather thongs tightly under his chin. His hands were very cold, and he went below for his gloves.

When he came out again, the snow was beginning to lie on the deck, and pile up against the masts. All the buccaneers were wearing their hoods, as he was.

There was a shout from Peran.

"Ice! There's a lump of ice dead ahead!"

The helmsman swung the wheel, and the ship turned a little to starboard. A great chunk of ice hit the portside of the ship. It didn't look very big at first glance, but Nicholas could see a mass of ice below the surface, pale green under the water.

He felt the ship shudder under his feet.

Then the ship pushed the ice to one side. It slid by, and was lost in the falling snow.

"Keep your eyes peeled, Peran!" shouted Barnabas Brandy. "We don't want to hit any more of those, if we can help it."

"I doubt if we'll be able to help it, Barnabas," said Captain Harken quietly. "That's why we strengthened the timbers, before we sailed *The Snow Goose* into the north. She'll stand a glancing blow — or I hope she will. But we mustn't hit any chunks of ice head-on — not even small ones."

The snow began to die away. The shower was over.

"Clear the decks!" cried Captain Harken.

The men seized brooms and short pieces of wood, and cleared the decks of snow, before it could harden into ice.

Nicholas took a broom, and worked with the others clearing the poop deck. When the ship was clear of snow, he put the broom away, and gazed out ahead.

He could see the white line of ice stretching right across the sea to the north.

"There's a whole field of ice ahead, Captain!" cried Peran, from the cross-trees. "There's nothing but ice, as far as I can see."

Captain Harken looked through his telescope.

"We'll go in a bit closer, before we turn," he said to Barnabas. "There may be a way through. Look at the clouds far to the north of us. They're dark. They must be over open water. If we can get through the ice, we'll find open sea on the far side."

"The wind's dropping," said Barnabas.

"Thank God for that," said Captain Harken.

"There's ice moving down towards us," cried Peran.

Even from the deck, they could see that the edges of the ice field were moving. Lanes of dark water were opening up.

As they came to the edge of the ice field, they saw a wide patch of open sea to the north-east. *The Snow Goose* sailed slowly towards it. Great rafts of ice began to drift past them on the dark sea.

By evening, the floating rafts of ice were all around them, but there was still a clear lane of water ahead. The clouds were higher. The wind had dropped, and the ship was scarcely moving. The dark sky to the north was a little nearer.

"Lower the boat!" cried Captain Harken. "We'll tow the ship through the ice field. There's safer water ahead."

"At least that will keep some of us warm!" said Barnabas Brandy.

It was very cold on deck. Nicholas had gone into the cabin to warm up from time to time, and he had helped the cooks to take mugs of hot soup around at midday. But he found that his fingers and toes were numb with cold, in spite of that. He wondered what it must be like for the men hauling the ropes and reefing the sails.

The boat was lowered into the water. A rope was slung across from the bows of the ship, and the buccaneers began to tow *The Snow Goose* through the ice.

They couldn't tow her in a straight line northwards. They had to follow the lanes of dark water between the ice, swinging now east and now west, moving towards the north whenever they could.

Captain Harken changed the rowers in the boat from time to time, and sent the men below for food and warmth. As the hours went on, he ordered a tot of rum for every man.

The dark cloud ahead came nearer and nearer. At last, Alwar, who was in the barrel at the cross-trees, shouted that he could see clear water to the north. (Peran had long since ended his watch at the foremast, and gone below. But Captain Harken kept one of the buccaneers in the cross-trees all the time, to watch for openings in the ice ahead.)

There was not much that he could do to help, but Nicholas kept coming out on deck to watch what was happening. From time to time, he helped the cooks to carry hot soup around to the men. From time to time, he helped to clear the deck of the broken bits of ice that fell from the rigging.

They were within sight of the far edge of the ice field, when Nicholas, looking over the rail of the ship, saw something that moved on a little island of ice, which was floating past to the east of them.

For a moment, he thought that it was one of the strange figures he had seen before, carved out of the ice by the wind. But it was cream-coloured, and it moved. For a moment, he was too startled to speak. And then his breath came back.

"There's a bear!" he cried. "A white bear! Over there on the ice!"

The buccaneers ran to the rail, and stared the way he was pointing.

The great bear moved out from behind a hummock on the ice, and stood there, staring at them. He was scarcely a hundred metres away.

A wide lane of water opened on their left.

"Port!" cried Captain Harken.

The ship swung to the left, along the lane of dark water, away from the bear.

"He's a big one!" cried Barnabas. "He must weigh as much as a small whale!"

"More than that," said Tom Gold. "He's the biggest bear I've ever seen."

Nicholas remembered the brown bear he had seen in The Strange Land. This one was even bigger.

The bear stood watching them for a few minutes. Then he plunged off the ice, into the water. Nicholas saw him swimming along, watching them. When the bear came to a patch of ice, he either pulled himself up on to it, and lumbered across it, or else he dived right down under it, and came up on the other side.

He didn't come towards the ship. He kept the same distance from it for a long time, watching the buccaneers. At last, he climbed out on to the ice again. He turned off towards the east, across a great island of ice.

"I shouldn't like to meet him on land!" exclaimed Barnabas, as the bear moved away. "Nor on a raft of floating ice!"

"No," said Tom Gold. "You wouldn't stand much chance against him. He could smash the jolly boat, too, if he wanted to. Even if you had a pistol, you'd have to kill him with the first shot. You wouldn't have time for a second. And I doubt if a pistol shot would kill him."

"We're safe enough on *The Snow Goose*," said Captain Harken. "But we're going to have to keep a sharp look-out, when we're in the jolly boat. And no one must go ashore alone."

They stood watching the bear, until at last they could see him no longer.

The clear water ahead was much nearer now, and before long the ship moved slowly out of the ice field.

The jolly boat was hauled in. The sails were set, and *The Snow Goose* sailed on across a calm sea.

A little wind began to blow. The clouds began to lift, and they saw the sun again.

Captain Harken sent Nicholas below. He was glad to go. Now that they were safely out of the ice, he felt very tired.

He took off his outer jacket in the great cabin, and ate some supper at the big table. (Supper? Or was it breakfast? Nicholas had been up for so long, that he wasn't sure.)

Then he went into the starboard cabin, and pulled off his boots and jacket. He lay down on the sack of straw just as he was, and wrapped the blankets around him.

A minute later, Nicholas was asleep.

Chapter 5
The scarlet berries

When Nicholas woke, he had no idea of the time. He looked out of the porthole. The sea was clear of ice, and the sun was shining low down in the sky. The sun had not gone down at all, all night. The clouds were red and gold, as if sunset and dawn were there at the same time.

The water in the jug in Nicholas's cabin had ice on it. He broke it, splashed a little on his face, and washed his hands. The water was so cold, that it made him gasp.

Nicholas dried himself, pulled a wooden comb through his hair, and put on his jacket.

He went into the great cabin. Captain Harken and Barnabas Brandy were sitting at the table, eating.

They greeted Nicholas cheerfully.

"You've slept the sun around, Nick!" cried Barnabas, taking a bite from a big hunk of bread, dipped in stew.

"How do you feel?" asked Captain Harken.

"Hungry!" said Nicholas.

Barnabas laughed. "Come and have supper," he said. "Cass has just brought it in. We might have known that you'd wake up just in time to eat!"

"Supper?" asked Nick.

"Breakfast, if you like," said Barnabas.

"It doesn't matter what you call it, up here

in the north,'' said Captain Harken. ''The sun didn't set at all last night. It was hidden by clouds for a time, but it didn't go down. It was like this when we were in the far south too, if you remember.''

''Why isn't there any ice on the sea at the moment, when we're so far north?'' asked Nicholas, sitting down at the table, and helping himself to meat stew and bread.

''We don't know the sea up here well enough to answer that,'' said Captain Harken. ''It must be something to do with the wind and the current.

''But there's plenty of ice about, as you'll see when you go on deck. There's a big field of ice, over to the west. We're sailing along the edge of it.

''There's land, too, on the far side of the ice.''

''Are we going there?'' asked Nicholas.

Captain Harken shook his head.

''No,'' he said, ''we're not. And you'll see why, as soon as you go on deck. We couldn't get through the ice field, even if we wanted to. And I don't think we need try. The land is covered with ice and snow. The scarlet berries may be called snow-berries, but I don't think anything could grow there.

''We're going to turn east for a bit soon. There's land over there, too. We'll see what we can find in that direction.''

''What makes you think there's land to the east, Francis?'' asked Barnabas.

"There must be," said Captain Harken. "You can tell that, from the way the ice is moving south. And the icebergs. They must be formed on some kind of land, and break off, when they reach the sea.

"There are little rocks on some of them, too. Haven't you noticed? They come from somewhere. I don't think the ice is all coming from the west and north. The main current comes down from the north, and we're sailing against it up some kind of wide channel, with land on either side of us.

"We'll turn east, and see what we can find."

Captain Harken pushed back his chair.

"I'm going on deck, Barnabas," he said. "You'd better get some rest."

"I don't need it," said Barnabas. "But you do."

Captain Harken shook his head. "You'll take four hours, Barnabas," he said. "That's an order. You can come up and take over then, when you've had some sleep."

He went out on deck.

Barnabas sighed. "Well, an order is an order, Nick," he said. "I'd better get some sleep. But keep an eye on the captain when you're on deck. See that he gets hot soup in a couple of hours time. He won't rest himself until he's sure the ship is clear of the ice, and he'll need something to keep him going. He's been on deck for hours."

Barnabas went into the starboard cabin.

Nicholas finished his stew, and went on deck.

They were still sailing north, along the edge of a great field of ice, but the water to the east was almost clear.

To the west, beyond the ice, Nicholas could see mountains and hills, white against the grey sky. Here and there he could see the dark rock of cliffs, jutting out into the sea. But the top of the cliffs, and the land beyond, was covered in ice and snow.

Ahead of the ship, beyond the ice field, he could see a big island, with a great headland running out into the sea. The cliffs there were free of ice, and the water below the headland was clear, too.

"Have a look through the spy-glass, Nicholas," said Captain Harken's voice at his side.

He turned, and saw the captain standing beside him.

"Thank you," he said, taking the telescope.

Through the telescope, the land looked even more frozen than before.

He moved the telescope down, and looked along the edge of the ice field.

On one of the rafts of floating ice, he saw a big brown shape. For a moment he thought it was a rock, and then he saw that the creature had two long white tusks.

"There's a walrus!" he cried. "There, on the ice!"

"Let's have the spy-glass, Nicholas," said Captain Harken, taking the telescope, and looking through it. "Now, where is this — walrus, did you call it?"

"On a bit of ice — just at the edge of the ice field," said Nicholas.

"I've got it," said Captain Harken. "It's like a great seal, with two tusks."

"It is a walrus," said Nicholas. "At least, I think it is."

"Have you seen one before?" asked Captain Harken, still looking.

"Not in real life," said Nicholas. "I've seen pictures." Now that he knew where it was, he could see the brown shape with his naked eye.

The walrus slithered across to the edge of the ice, and heaved itself down into the water.

"I've never seen a creature like that before," said Captain Harken. "But I've heard of seals with tusks. There's a story about a seal's tusk that Hornwollen is supposed to have had with him, once.

"Well, 'walrus' is as good a name as any. It's shorter than 'tusked seal', and a lot easier to say. We'll call it a walrus.

"We're going to turn east, as soon as we've reached the headland. Keep your eyes open, and let me know if you see any more of them. Seals, too. I saw some seals on the ice earlier, when you were sleeping."

Captain Harken went up on to the poop deck. They passed the northern edge of the ice field, and sailed on, towards the high cliffs of the headland. The cliffs were at the end of a long arm of land which jutted out into the sea.

Nicholas heard a cry above his head. He looked up, and saw some seabirds flying over the ship. The birds circled all around them, as if they were looking them over. Then they wheeled away towards the headland, and were lost in the distance.

As the ship sailed in under the cliffs, Nicholas saw the birds again, high up on the rock.

The cliffs towered up out of the sea, far above their heads. At the end of the headland there were two great pillars of rock, standing like dark twin towers in the sea.

The sheer cliffs of the headland stretched back towards the land. They were free of snow, but where they joined the island, the land was capped with ice.

As they came closer, more birds flew out from the cliffs, wheeling in the air above their heads.

Nicholas went down to the cook's galley, below the main deck, and asked for a mug of soup for the captain.

The cook gave him a steaming mug, and he took it up to the poop deck, where Captain Harken was watching the cliffs through his telescope.

Captain Harken lowered the telescope for a moment, saw him, and laughed.

"So you're keeping me going, Nicholas, are you?" he said. "Well, I shall be glad of some hot soup."

He took the mug, and drank a little.

"They're strange cliffs," he said to Tom Gold, who was standing beside him. "They look like natural cliffs, and yet in places you'd almost think someone had been at work on them."

He handed the telescope to Tom Gold. "Do you see those caves, at the top? Some are just slits, but some are almost square. You'd think they might be windows in a giant castle."

"They must be caves," said Tom Gold, looking through the telescope. "I can see birds flying in and out of them."

He handed back the telescope. Captain Harken finished his soup, and looked through it again.

"I expect you're right," he said. "They must be just caves. They couldn't be anything else. And anyway, there's no chance of looking at them more closely. We can't land.

"We'd better sail east. There's land over there, too, and the sea is almost clear of ice in that direction."

The Snow Goose turned eastwards. An hour or so later, Captain Harken went below and Barnabas Brandy came on deck.

"There's an island out there ahead of us," said Barnabas Brandy, looking through Captain Harken's telescope. "We'll keep south of that. Would you like to have a look, Nick?''

He handed Nicholas the telescope.

Nicholas looked through it, and saw a great, pointed rock rising up out of the sea.

''It looks more like a giant's hat than an island,'' he said.

Barnabas laughed. ''So it does,'' he said, taking back the telescope. ''We'll be careful to keep clear of it.''

He looked at Nicholas, and saw that he was shivering.

''Better go below, Nick,'' he said. ''There's no need for you to freeze on deck.''

Nicholas was feeling very cold. He was feeling tired, too. He didn't want to miss anything, but he thought he would go down for a while. When he got to the cabin, the warmth made him sleepy. He took off his outer clothes, rolled himself up in his blankets, and lay down on his straw mattress in the starboard cabin.

* * *

He woke to find Halek shaking him by the shoulder.

''If you're going to sleep for the rest of the voyage, Nick, just tell me,'' said Halek, as Nicholas opened his eyes. ''But you're going to miss a lot.''

''What's happening?'' asked Nicholas, sitting up and throwing off the blankets.

"We're near land," said Halek. "And what's more, it's free of snow, and the captain can see plants growing on it. There's a boat going ashore, to look for snow-berries. Do you want to come?"

"You bet I do," said Nicholas, pulling on his boots.

He struggled into his jacket, and grabbed his gloves. He put on his outside jacket as he went into the great cabin with Halek.

There was food on the table but Nicholas hadn't time to eat any.

By the time they got on deck, the jolly boat was in the water. There were six men at the oars, and Barnabas Brandy was in the stern.

"Come on, you two, look alive!" cried Barnabas, as Halek and Nicholas reached the ship's rail. "We can't wait all day!"

"It was my fault," said Nicholas, as he climbed down the rope ladder into the boat. "I was asleep. Halek woke me."

"Sleeping again!" said Barnabas. "You sleep longer than a toad in winter!

"Sit down, boy, sit down! Don't rock the boat! Are you in Halek? All clear? All right, give way."

The buccaneers bent to the oars, and the boat moved in towards the shore.

The sun was low in the sky. It shone on the land ahead, and they could see that there was a little stony beach, with a steep slope behind it. Much farther off, the land rose steeply to a high ridge of rock. It looked green and brown in the golden sunshine.

They pulled the boat in close to some rocks, and climbed out. Peran tied the painter (the rope in the bows) to a rock.

Barnabas handed Nicholas a piece of paper, and a horn slung on a leather thong.

"Here's one of the horns Sorn gave us, before we left The Strange Land, Nick," he said. "Captain Harken said that every man going ashore must carry one. Blow it, if you need any help, or if you find snow-berries.

"There's a drawing of a snow-berry on that bit of paper. Everyone's got a copy. That's what we're looking for.

"There's one other thing. The water is calm just now, but Captain Harken thinks we may get a bit of wind soon, and there's a fog bank lying out to sea. If the wind gets up, or the fog moves in, he'll fire the cannon on *The Snow Goose.* If you hear the cannon, come straight back to the boat. Don't wait for anything. Even if you've found a whole field full of snow-berries, leave them, and make for the shore."

"All right," said Nicholas, taking the horn and hanging it around his neck. He looked carefully at the drawing of the snow-berry, and then pushed it into his pocket.

"Let's get up this bank, and see what the land is like at the top of it," said Barnabas.

They began to climb up the steep slope.

Nicholas gazed at the ground in surprise. It

was covered with growing plants. He knew that they had come north towards the end of summer, but he had seen so much snow and ice covering the ground, that he was surprised by the colours under his feet.

In places, the grey rock was covered by patches of bright orange, or pale green. There was some kind of black moss between the stones, and all kinds of little plants were growing. None of them was more than three or four centimetres high. There were some very small ones rather like buttercups, and there were little white flowers. There were patches of beautiful red leaves, and a plant with little twigs of wood, and bright orange leaves. There were some plants with yellow leaves and blue berries, and some with green leaves and scarlet berries.

When he saw these, Nicholas pulled the drawing out of his pocket, and looked at it again. But the berries were not the scarlet berries he was looking for. The leaves were the wrong shape.

When they came to the top of the steep slope, they saw the high ridge of rock against the sky, some way away. The land in between was fairly flat, with little hummocks here and there. It rose up steeply again to the ridge, about a mile away from where they were standing. The whole place was covered with plants.

"We're going to have to search the

ground," said Barnabas Brandy. "This is just the kind of place where we might find snow-berries.

"Spread out in a long line. We'll work our way over to that ridge."

The buccaneers spread out widely, and began to move slowly across towards the ridge.

Nicholas was at the end of the line, on the far left. Then came Halek, and then the other buccaneers, strung out as far as they could go.

Nicholas looked at every patch of growing plants, to see if there were berries on them. Every now and then, he pulled the drawing out of his pocket, to make sure that he knew what he was looking for. Time went on, and he found nothing like the plant in the drawing.

The ground in front of him suddenly dropped steeply into a gully. A little stream was running along the floor of the gully, twenty or thirty metres below him.

Nicholas looked up, thinking that he must call out to Halek, and tell him about it. But Halek was a long way away, to his right. Barnabas Brandy was still farther to the right, and he was pointing forwards.

Nicholas looked across to the ridge, and saw something white moving on the hillside. It wasn't big enough for a bear, and as he watched, it stopped, and sat up.

It was a white hare.

Nicholas looked along the side of the steep slope ahead. He could see three other hares, higher up. They were sitting there, just below the ridge, watching the buccaneers.

As he looked at them, the first hare ran up to join the others, and all four went off together, over the top of the ridge and out of sight.

Nicholas looked over towards Halek. Halek was even farther off than before.

He looked down into the gully. There were some little patches of snow still lying here and there in the bottom, on the edge of the stream. He thought he could see a clump of pale yellow and bright red leaves in the middle of a large patch of snow.

"I'll just go down and see what that is," he said to himself. He clambered down over the edge of the gully towards the stream.

He reached the patch of snow, and looked down. A clump of pale yellow leaves, about a metre long, was growing right in the middle of the snow. Bright red berries showed among the yellow leaves.

Nicholas drew in his breath in excitement. He pulled the drawing out of his pocket, and dropped down beside the berries.

The berries and the leaves looked exactly like the drawing in his hand.

He had found the scarlet berries of the snow.

Chapter 6
Hornwollen

Boom!

The sound of the cannon on *The Snow Goose* echoed against the rocks.

Nicholas looked up, startled. Grey mist was blowing across the top of the gully. He had been staring so hard at the ground, looking first for snow-berries, and then at the hares, that he had not thought of keeping a watch behind him. He had never thought that the fog might be moving in from the sea.

He bent down quickly, and picked two or three of the scarlet berries and yellow leaves. He was sure that he had found the right ones, but he wanted to be able to prove it.

Then he scrambled up the side of the gully.

It was steeper than he had thought, and once or twice he slipped back. By the time he reached the top, a thick fog had rolled in across the land.

Nicholas stared about him. He could no longer see even the floor of the gully. The thick, grey mist blew around him on every side. He heard faint sounds of horns, blowing far away. The buccaneers must be going back to the beach.

He pulled out his own horn, and blew it. The far off horns sounded faintly in reply.

Nicholas thought that he knew which way to go, and he set off into the fog. He struggled on for what seemed a long time. Just as he was beginning to think that he must be near the shore, the ground began to rise, and he knew that he must have turned the wrong way.

He lifted his horn again, and blew. The sound echoed against the far ridge.

He listened. There was no answering horn.

Nicholas blew the horn again, and then again.

Silence.

Nicholas sat down to think. Something must have happened. It couldn't only be the fog, or the buccaneers would be looking for him. He must have been going the wrong way. He got up, and started back, down the gentle slope. The wind was growing stronger. Perhaps it would blow the fog away.

It seemed to Nicholas that he had been wandering about in the fog for a long time, when he came to the edge of the gully again. It was not the same place where he had climbed down before, but he guessed that it was the same gully, because he could hear running water below him. He was feeling thirsty, and he decided to climb down, and get a drink.

The fog was a little thinner now. He scrambled down the side of the gully, and found the stream. It was pouring down over the rocks in a little waterfall. He pulled off his gloves, bent down, and cupped his hands. The water was as cold as ice. It was wonderful to drink, but it made his hands numb.

He was just putting on his gloves again, when he heard a wild cry. It came from somewhere quite close to him, a little way downstream. Someone had cried out in fear or pain.

Nicholas turned, and ran along the edge of the stream towards the sound, jumping from rock to rock. The stream bent sharply to his left, round a little jutting cliff. He turned the corner, and stopped dead.

A man was crouching by a rock, only a few metres away from him, and just beyond him stood a great white bear.

Nicholas stood as if turned into stone. His thoughts flew back to a time when he had been in The Strange Land with Captain Rasha, and a great brown bear had come lumbering out of the trees. This bear was even bigger. Fear swept over him, and for one terrible moment, he couldn't move.

Then he remembered what Captain Rasha had said. "If you want to frighten a bear away, you have to make him think that you're stronger and bigger than he is. The bigger and deeper a bellow you can give, the more likely the bear is to run away." It was almost as if he could hear Captain Rasha speaking.

The bear reared up on its back legs. Its eyes were on Nicholas. Nicholas knew that he couldn't manage a very big bellow, but he had the horn. He ran forward, and leapt up on to the rock, so that he seemed taller than the bear. He gripped the horn, and blew with all his might.

The horn blared out. It seemed louder than he had ever heard it before. The sides of the gully echoed with the sound.

The bear dropped down on to all four feet again.

Nicholas blew the horn again, and again the sound echoed against the sides of the gully.

Slowly, the bear turned. It lumbered off into the mist.

Nicholas climbed down from the rock, and leant back against it. His knees were shaking so much that he could hardly stand.

"Well done, boy! Well done!"

He looked down. The man was sitting on the ground looking up at him. In his excitement over the bear, Nicholas had almost forgotten him.

"Do you think the bear's gone?" he asked, in rather a shaky voice.

"Yes, he's gone," said the man. "You've frightened him off. It's a good thing you had that horn, or we'd both have been dead.

"Who are you, and where in all the seas do you come from?"

Nicholas looked at him. He was an old man. He had a white beard, and shaggy white eyebrows, and he looked very weather-beaten. He was dressed in white, in a thick jacket and hood, with long, white boots pulled up over his trousers.

"My name's Nicholas — or Nick," Nicholas said. "And I'm with Captain Harken. We've come from Ramir. Our ship's called *The Snow Goose*."

"From Ramir?" questioned the old man in surprise. "What are you doing here, so far north?"

"We've come to find snow-berries," said Nicholas, "the scarlet berries of the snow. There's been a terrible illness in Ramir. People are dying. Only the snow-berries cure them, and they have used all they had. So Captain Harken has come up north, to find some more, if he can."

"So that's what it is!" exclaimed the man. "Thank God for that. The People of the Snow were afraid you might be here after whales."

"The People of the Snow!" cried Nicholas. "Do you know them? Are you one of them?"

"I know them, but I'm not one of them," said the man. "I'm a wanderer. I came from Ramir myself once, long ago. So long ago, that they will have forgotten me in Ramir. I came north with the Arcons. My name is Hornwollen, and I'm one of those who wander all over the earth."

"Hornwollen!" cried Nicholas. "You gave the snow-berries to a man called Barka."

Hornwollen stared at him.

"How do you know that?" he asked.

"Barka took the snow-berries to Ramir," said Nicholas. "He sold them there. They were the only berries they had, when everyone became ill.''

''Is Barka on *The Snow Goose*?'' asked Hornwollen.

''He's dead,'' said Nicholas. ''He got drunk, and fell in the sea. No one knew where the berries came from, except that they grew in the north. So Captain Harken sailed north in *The Snow Goose,* to try to find them — or you. He wanted to find you.''

''Well! That's a strange thing!'' said Hornwollen. ''I came here today, gathering snow-berries. I've been in the gully for hours. I didn't see the ship come in, but I heard the cannon fire. But by that time the fog had come down, and I could see nothing.

''And then I slipped and fell, and hurt my foot. I cried out, and the bear came out of the mist. I thought that was the end of me! And then there you were, leaping up on the rock and blowing that horn until my ears rang with the sound of it!

''You've saved my life, Nicholas — and your own, too. Give me a hand now, and I'll see if I can get back to my boat.''

Nicholas stepped forward, and held out his hand.

Hornwollen took it, and pulled himself up. He was so thin and light that Nicholas had no difficulty in helping him. Hornwollen stood leaning back against the rock, standing on one leg.

He rested the other foot on the ground, and

tried to see if he could put a little weight on it.

Nicholas could see that it was painful.

"I'll have to strap it up, as tight as I can," said Hornwollen. "And then — can you give me a hand down to my boat? Where are the other men from your ship?"

"They must have gone back," said Nicholas. "The cannon was a signal from the ship. I tried to go back, too, but I turned the wrong way in the fog."

"Won't they come and look for you?" asked Hornwollen.

"They will if they can," said Nicholas. "Something must have happened to stop them."

Hornwollen nodded. "I can tell you what has happened," he said. "The ice will have moved in. I know this place. I know the sea up here, and the way the wind and the currents move the ice. I came over here today, because I could tell that there was a change coming, and I wanted to gather as many berries as I could, before the snow came.

"Any captain would have to move his ship out to sea, so that she wouldn't be caught in the ice. He'd have to do that, even if he left someone on land. He's got to think of the lives of everyone on board.

"He'll come back for you as soon as he can, I expect. But he'd have to move out a bit."

"Will the sea freeze?" asked Nicholas.

"Not just yet," said Hornwollen. "You may have a bit of time yet. But the ship will have to turn south soon.

"Now — give me that pack over there Nicholas, would you? Over there, by that sack."

Nicholas looked the way Hornwollen was pointing, and saw two patches of white among the rocks. For a moment, he thought they were snow, but when he looked carefully, he could see from the shape that one was a pack, with straps, and one a sack. He went over, picked up the pack, and brought it across to Hornwollen. It was surprisingly light.

Hornwollen sat down on a rock and opened the pack. He took out a knife, and a big square of white cloth. He cut the cloth into strips with the knife.

Then he pulled off his boot. He was wearing thick white socks. He took his sock off, too, and tied the strips tightly around his ankle and foot. Then he pulled on the sock, and eased his foot back into the boot again. The boot was made of the same soft, white material as his jacket. It was laced in front, so that, by letting out the laces, he could get it on.

Nicholas helped him to his feet again. Hornwollen tested his foot on the ground, and then nodded.

"I can manage, if you can give me a shoulder to lean on," he said. "Could you carry my pack, too?''

''Yes,'' said Nicholas. ''It's very light. What about the sack?''

''The sack's full of snow-berries,'' said Hornwollen. ''It's not heavy, but we'll have to leave it. You can't carry everything.''

''We mustn't leave snow-berries!'' exclaimed Nicholas.

''I've plenty of them for myself, and the People of the Snow,'' said Hornwollen, ''but I expect you'll want all you can get for Ramir. Very well. We'll have to move in stages. We'll go a little way, and then you can come back and get the sack. Then we'll go on again. This way. We'll go down the gully by the stream. Then we can't get lost, even in the fog.''

They set off slowly, along the bank of the little stream. Nicholas helped the old man along for twenty or thirty metres. Then Hornwollen rested, while Nicholas went back for the sack of snow-berries. Then they went another thirty metres, and again Nicholas went back for the sack.

It was slow going, but Hornwollen needed to rest his foot, and Nicholas didn't want to leave snow-berries behind. He knew how much they were needed in Ramir.

The fog was much thinner now, but they kept down in the gully, and Nicholas had only to follow the stream, to find his way.

At last, the gully opened out, and they came to the beach.

They were on the other side of the rocks where the buccaneers had landed. There was a little cove, with a beach of large pebbles, between two little cliffs of rock which stretched out into the sea.

A boat had been pulled up on the beach. It was rather like a canoe, with covered ends. A long double paddle, of the kind Nicholas had seen in pictures of Eskimos, lay in the boat.

Nicholas helped Hornwollen down to the edge of the shore. Then he pushed the boat down beside him. It was made of some kind of very thin metal, and it was surprisingly light.

Hornwollen leant forward, supporting himself on the boat. Nicholas dropped the pack and the sack into it, and helped Hornwollen to push the boat out, and climb in.

When they were both safely sitting in it, Hornwollen took the paddle, and they moved out from the shore.

They were only a few metres out, when they came to the ice. The sea was full of it. Great rafts of ice were everywhere. Some of them were like little icebergs, carved into strange shapes. Some were white, and some chunks of floating ice were bright blue.

But there were still narrow lanes of dark water between them, and Hornwollen drove the boat forward westwards. Sometimes they had to go towards the north, and sometimes towards the south, to get round islands of ice, but they gradually moved west, out to sea.

The mist was much thinner now. It was thicker on the water than it was overhead. Overhead, Nicholas could see through the mist that the sky was blue. He would soon have been lost, had he been on his own, but Hornwollen seemed to know exactly which way to go.

After a long time, Nicholas saw what he thought was a thicker, darker patch of mist ahead. As they came closer to it, he saw that it was an island.

A great rock rose up in front of them. It was tall and pointed, with very steep sides. Nicholas recognised it. It was the island he had seen from the ship, just before he had gone below to sleep.

As they came towards it, he saw that there was flatter rock at the base, so that the island really did look like an immense, pointed hat, with its brim resting on the sea.

Hornwollen drove the boat into a narrow little harbour, cut out of the rock.

"Climb out, Nicholas," he said. "This is where I live."

Nicholas stared at him for a moment. He could see nothing but bare rock on every side. He climbed out without a word.

Hornwollen handed him the pack, and the sack of berries, and then climbed out himself. He crawled on to the rock on his knees, to save his foot, while Nicholas held the boat steady.

Together, they pulled the boat up out of the water.

Nicholas helped Hornwollen to his feet.

"This way," said Hornwollen, leaning on Nicholas's shoulder. He limped across to the great point of rock, which rose up in front of them.

Hornwollen bent down and lifted up a stone. Nicholas saw a silver lever sticking up out of the rock at his feet.

Hornwollen pulled the lever back.

A stone door swung open at the foot of the great cone of rock ahead of them.

As the door opened, a big dog shot out of the doorway, barking in delight, and ran up to Hornwollen. Then he saw Nicholas, and his bark changed. His hair rose, making him look bigger than ever.

"It's all right, Kuluk, he's a friend!" said Hornwollen.

Kuluk's hair slowly flattened down again. Nicholas stood quite still, while the dog sniffed him.

Kuluk's tail gave a slow wag, and Hornwollen laughed.

"You'll be safe enough now," he said. "Kuluk is one of the dogs I brought with me, when I came to the north. He lives here with me still.

"I gave the others to the People of the Snow, and they keep them in their mountain home, to pull their sledges in the winter. But I kept Kuluk here with me.

"Come in. Kuluk won't hurt you."

They went through the door. Hornwollen pulled another lever, which was on the rock wall, just inside, and the door closed behind them.

Nicholas stood still, staring all around him.

They were standing in a great, round room. The walls were of rock. Light came in through slits in the rock, higher up. There were silver lanterns, too, hanging from brackets around the walls. They lit up the whole room, with a silvery light which reminded Nicholas of the lantern on the bows of *The Silver Dolphin*.

There was a bed against one wall, covered with sheepskins. There was a wooden table in the middle, with three or four chairs pushed under it. Over at one side, across from the bed, there were several big, wooden armchairs. The chairs, too, were covered with sheepskins.

There were three big cupboards against the walls of the room, and two large wooden chests, bound with silver.

A narrow strip of silver metal ran all the way around the walls, about a metre above the floor.

At one side, a flight of stone steps led up out of the room, into the darkness above.

Hornwollen took off his jacket. Nicholas had been too surprised by what he saw to think about the cold, but he suddenly realised that he was warm. He untied his hood, pushed it back, and took off his own outer jacket. Kuluk sniffed the jacket carefully, and wagged his tail again.

Hornwollen looked at Nicholas, and laughed.

"You look as if you can't believe your eyes," he said. "That's the way I looked, when I first saw the houses of the People of the Snow."

"Do the People of the Snow live in places like this?" gasped Nicholas.

"They live in much finer places than this," said Hornwollen. "But this is one of their smaller houses. They have given it to me, while I'm here in the north."

"But — but what is the light? And where does the warmth come from?" asked Nicholas.

"They dig strange metals out of the rocks," said Hornwollen. "They forge them in their furnaces. They make the silver lanterns from them — lanterns that never go out. The warmth comes from that strip of silver metal around the wall.

"I don't understand how it works. It's part of their magic."

"Can they disappear, as people say?" asked Nicholas. "The Arcons said that they vanish into the snow."

Hornwollen laughed. "They disappear," he said, "but they don't vanish."

"What do you mean?" asked Nicholas.

"They make this white, silvery cloth, that

shines, and looks like the snow. They dress in it, as I do.

"If you are wearing clothes made of this cloth, and you don't want anyone to see you, all you have to do is to turn your back, and lie down against a rock. Then you look just like a patch of snow. If you curl up, so that they can't see your shape, people will think you are just another snowdrift.

"The People of the Snow don't vanish — but if they hide in the snow, you can't see them.

"Come. Help me over to a chair."

He put his hand on Nicholas's shoulder, and limped over to one of the armchairs.

Kuluk walked across the room beside them, and lay down.

"Now bring me the jar of white ointment, which you'll find in that cupboard," said Hornwollen.

Nicholas did as he was asked. Hornwollen took off his boot and sock, untied the bandage and rubbed the ointment into his foot. Then he tied the foot up again.

He changed his boots for soft shoes.

"We'll have supper," he said, "and then we'll think about what we should do next."

"Shouldn't we keep a look-out for Captain Harken and *The Snow Goose*?" asked Nicholas.

Hornwollen shook his head.

"There's nothing we can do about *The Snow Goose* yet, Nicholas," he said. "They have gone southwards, and the ice is too thick for them to get back. They'll have to wait for a day or two, before the ice moves again.

"Do you think they will come back for you? By the time the ice clears, they'll think you've frozen to death. There's cold weather coming — colder than it's been before. It won't be long before the sea begins to freeze.

"But don't be afraid. The snow people will send you south, if you want to go. Or you can spend the winter here, and go south in the spring."

"Captain Harken will come back if he can," said Nicholas. "He'll come back for the snow-berries."

"Most of the berries grow in the gully," said Hornwollen. "There are a few plants along the shore, but the buccaneers may not have found them. Will Captain Harken come back for you?"

"He will if he can — if he thinks I'm still there," said Nicholas.

"What do you mean — if he thinks you're still there?"

"I — I come from somewhere else," said Nicholas. "I come through a silver ring, from another country — another world. It's difficult to explain. But Captain Harken may think I've gone back through the ring."

Hornwollen stared at him.

"Have you heard of Jeremy Strange?" he asked.

"He's my great-uncle," said Nicholas. "He gave me the ring."

"Ah!" said Hornwollen. "Now I understand. I met Jeremy Strange in the far east. He told me about the ring.

"So that's who you are, and that's where you come from!

"But where's Jeremy? Is he still alive?"

"Yes," said Nicholas. "He lives in Ramir all the time. He's staying on an island just now, with Solomon Dee."

"Well, that *is* news," said Hornwollen. "Jeremy Strange! I remember him so well. But I can see what might happen, Nicholas. If Captain Harken thinks you have gone back through the silver ring, he won't risk his ship to try to rescue you."

Nicholas nodded, rather unhappily. That was one of the difficulties about being in Ramir. The buccaneers didn't always know when he had gone back through the ring.

"We'd better go across to the rock castles as soon as we can," said Hornwollen. "The People of the Snow will help us. If the ice moves in, *The Snow Goose* may need their help too, whether they come back for you or not.

"We'll have supper, Nicholas, and then we must rest for a few hours. But we won't sleep for long. We'll set out across to the rock castles, and tell the People of the Snow what's happening.

"You see that cupboard over there? You'll find some food inside it, and a little stove.

Bring them over here to the table, and we'll have supper. There's a bowl of food for Kuluk too. He'll be hungry."

Nicholas went over to the cupboard. There was a metal pot, with some fish stew in it, and a small stove. A bowl full of scraps of meat stood on a shelf on its own.

He carried everything across to the table, and went back for some bread and a big round cheese, and some bowls full of berries.

Hornwollen handed him the bowl of scraps.

"Give Kuluk his supper," he said. "If you give that to him, he'll know you're really a friend!"

Nicholas put the bowl down on the ground, and Kuluk wolfed the meat. When it was all gone, he licked his lips, and lay down again by Hornwollen.

Hornwollen took the stove, and lit it by pulling a lever. The stove didn't light in the usual way. A piece of silver metal in it glowed suddenly very bright.

As soon as the stew was hot, they had supper.

Nicholas was very glad of something to eat. He had been thinking so hard about *The Snow Goose* and Hornwollen and Captain Harken, that he had forgotten how hungry he was. But when he saw the food, his mouth watered, and he felt very empty indeed.

After supper, they lay down for a few hours, to sleep. They were both very tired.

"I'll wake you before long," said Hornwollen, as Kuluk settled down beside him. "We'll go across to the rock castles, and see the People of the Snow. But sleep now. You must rest, and so must I."

Chapter 7
Across the icy sea

Captain Harken, Tom Gold and Barnabas Brandy, were standing on the deck of *The Snow Goose,* staring into the mist.

Great rafts of ice were all around the ship. She was moving slowly through the water, shouldering the ice to one side as she went. A wide lane of dark water lay ahead. Captain Harken had called in the jolly boat, which had been towing the ship. There was a light wind from the north, and there was just enough room between the ice-floes for them to sail. Every now and then *The Snow Goose* struck a piece of ice a glancing blow, and the ship shuddered with the force of it. But she sailed slowly on.

They had been sailing south for some hours. The great field of floating ice was still around them, but the lanes of open water were growing wider.

"I should never have come back without the boy," said Barnabas Brandy, staring out over the ship's side.

"You had to, Barnabas," said Captain Harken. "You were in command of the shore party. You had to bring them back, when the ice came in, and we fired the cannon. You had their lives to think about. You waited as long as you could. You couldn't send them off into the fog, looking for Nicholas. You'd all have been lost."

''I should have sent them back, and stayed myself,'' said Barnabas.

Captain Harken shook his head.

''The boat only just got back to the ship as it was,'' he said. ''They'd never have done it without you.''

''I've never left anyone behind before,'' said Barnabas.

''We don't know whether you've left anyone now, Barnabas,'' said Captain Harken. ''We don't know whether Nicholas is there or not. You couldn't stay, and risk all the men's lives looking for Nicholas, when you knew he might have gone back to his own world. You know that he may have gone back through the silver ring.''

''I only hope he has!'' said Barnabas.

''There's a bear!'' shouted Cass, who was in the cross-trees. ''There's a bear on the ice! Over on the starboard bow!''

They looked out to starboard. Through the mist, they could see a great white bear, standing on a raft of ice. The bear was staring at the ship. He slid over the edge of the ice, swam across a gap, and pulled himself out on the far side. He looked back at the ship again for a moment, and then turned and went off across the ice, into the fog.

''That's another thing I'm afraid of for the boy,'' said Barnabas. ''Bears.''

''Did you see any on the shore?'' asked Captain Harken.

''We saw some footprints,'' said Barnabas.

"It's no good, Barnabas," said Captain Harken. "There's nothing we can do for the moment. We've got to get *The Snow Goose* out of this ice field.

"But when the ship's clear, I'm going to take the boat back. You found one little plant of snow-berries, too. Where there is one plant, there may be more. We can row a boat through most of the ice field. And if the sea freezes up, we'll pull it out and haul it over the ice."

"You'll let me take it?" asked Barnabas.

Captain Harken shook his head.

"Not this time, Barnabas," he said. "I'll leave you and Tom Gold in command of the ship, and take six volunteers with me."

"But I'm the one who left Nicholas behind!" cried Barnabas.

"I'm not just going for the boy," said Captain Harken. "It's the only place where there's a chance of finding more snow-berries. I don't think the winter has closed in yet. The ice is drifting down from the north, but there may still be clear water behind it. We'll turn east soon. If you find clear water, you can sail her north again, to meet us. But we must explore that open ground, where you found that plant growing, before the snow comes.

"It will be dangerous, I know, and I can't ask for volunteers to go back, unless I go myself. So I shall take the boat. You'll stay in charge of *The Snow Goose,* with Tom Gold to help you. That's an order, Barnabas. But we'll see if we can get into clearer water, first.

"Let me see that plant again."

Barnabas went into the cabin, and came back with a small plant. It had yellow leaves, and scarlet berries.

"That's what we're looking for," said Captain Harken, taking it from him. "We must get back, if we can."

* * *

It was some hours later, when Peran shouted from the cross-trees: "Clear water ahead! A great lake of it!"

The fog had turned to mist, and the mist was lifting. The sky was blue above them. They could see fields of floating ice far over to the left and right of them, but the sea ahead was clear. As they watched, the last of the mist drifted up into the sky.

"We'll go now," said Captain Harken. "Tack the ship back and forth for as long as you can, Barnabas. And if the sea opens up to the north, sail back to meet us. But don't take any chances. We'll come back south to *The Snow Goose,* one way or another — by sea, or over the ice.

"Wait two weeks for us. If we're not here in two weeks, or if the sea begins to freeze or more ice drifts down, sail south for Ramir. That's an order, too.

"If the worst comes to the worst, and

you've gone, we'll try to make our way down to the Arcons, and spend the winter with them."

Barnabas nodded. "I won't wreck *The Snow Goose*," he said. "But don't stay up there too long, Francis. And don't kill yourself, looking for the boy — or the berries."

"I shall have six men with me," said Captain Harken. "I've their lives to think of, too."

The jolly boat was ready. Warm, sheepskin sleeping bags had been rolled up and tied, and put into her, with plenty of food. When Captain Harken had asked for volunteers, everyone wanted to go. He chose Downalong, Cass, Peran, Alwar and two others. They were all dressed in the clothes the buccaneers had worn when they were in the far south: skins, sewn together so that the hair of one skin was inside, and the other on the outside. They were much warmer than the woollen clothes they had been wearing.

Tom Gold was left behind, to act as first mate. Halek wasn't chosen, because he was not yet as strong as a full-grown man. The strongest men were needed, in case they had to haul the boat over the ice.

The buccaneers lowered the boat into the water. The wind was against them, but it was very light. They had a sail with them, as well as oars, in case they could use it later.

Captain Harken climbed down into the

boat with the others, and they moved slowly off, back towards the north.

Barnabas Brandy and Tom Gold stood with Halek and the other buccaneers on the deck of *The Snow Goose,* watching them go.

But before they were out of sight, Barnabas shouted some orders, and *The Snow Goose* began to move slowly through the water, on its first tack towards the west.

* * *

Farther north, Nicholas and Hornwollen were also making their way in a boat through the floating ice.

Hornwollen's boat had two paddles, and Nicholas sat in the front, using one of them, while Hornwollen sat at the back with the other.

They were making very good progress. The boat was wonderfully light, and Hornwollen knew just how to steer her through the ice.

Once, they came to such a large floating island of ice that Hornwollen brought them in alongside, and they lifted the boat out. Nicholas pulled her across the island, while Hornwollen limped beside him. They slid the boat into a lane of water on the far side. But most of the time they were able to find cracks of open water between the ice-floes.

They had set out after some hours of sleep, and another meal. They had left Kuluk behind, to his great disgust. But Hornwollen

planned to go back to him, as soon as he had taken Nicholas to the People of the Snow.

The fog had lifted, and they could see high cliffs ahead of them. They were coming towards the two great pillars of rock which Nicholas had seen before, when they had sighted the island from *The Snow Goose.* The two pillars towered up, like two great castles. They were at the end of a long point, stretching out into the sea. Behind them, the cliffs rose up out of the water, two hundred metres or more high.

As they came closer, Nicholas could see dark cracks and caves, high up in the cliffs. He remembered what Captain Harken had said, about some of the cracks and holes looking as if they had been carved out by men.

"We're nearly there, Nicholas," said Hornwollen. "These are the Twin Castles of the People of the Snow."

"The Twin Castles?" questioned Nicholas.

"That's what they call them," said Hornwollen.

"But they didn't build them," said Nicholas. "They're cliffs on an island."

"No, they didn't build them," said Hornwollen. "They hollowed them out. Wait until you see inside! And look — the watchers are still here. They'll be flying south any day now, but they haven't gone yet."

Nicholas looked up. He could see birds flying over the top of the cliffs.

"Those birds?" he asked. "Are they the watchers?"

"Yes," said Hornwollen. "Watchers, and messengers, too."

Nicholas remembered how Solomon Dee had sent messages by the birds.

Hornwollen steered the little boat to a flat rock at the bottom of one of the great cliff castles.

Nicholas scrambled out on to the rock, and then helped Hornwollen to climb out after him.

The rock sloped up out of the sea. They pulled the boat up after them, and Hornwollen made it fast to a silver ring, set in the rock.

"Now, you must help me to the door, Nicholas," said Hornwollen, "and after that, the snow people will have to carry me up. I can't manage the steps, until my foot is better."

"Steps?" questioned Nicholas.

"Inside the castle," said Hornwollen. "Come. Let us get to the door."

The rock sloped steeply up ahead of them to the foot of the great rock castle.

Hornwollen put his hand on Nicholas's shoulder, and limped across. When they reached the great rock, Hornwollen lifted a hollow stone. There was a silver lever under it, which he pulled.

Somewhere overhead, inside the great castle of rock, they heard a bell toll.

Chapter 8
The People of the Snow

A gap appeared in the rock wall. A door had opened, and Nicholas saw a man standing in the doorway.

Nicholas stared at him. His face and hands were brown, and his head, which was bare, was covered with curly brown hair. He was wearing a white tunic, over white trousers, which were bound by silver thongs, rather like the trousers worn by the Arcons.

"Hornwollen!" he cried stepping forward. "Who is this? What has happened, that you bring a stranger to our castle?"

"You must forgive me, Kell," said Hornwollen. "The boy was lost, and in need of help. He saved me from a bear. He'll do you no harm. He is already my friend.

"I must take him to the Ecrun at once. But you'll have to help me. I fell and twisted my foot, and I cannot get up your stairs."

"I must go to the Ecrun first," said Kell. "Wait in here, while I tell him that you have come."

He helped Hornwollen through the door into the rock castle.

Nicholas followed. He found himself standing in a room cut out of the rock. It was rather like the room in Hornwollen's house. Silver lanterns hung from the wall, and it was heated by a band of silver metal. A flight of steps on one side of the room led up into the rock castle.

There were two chairs, covered in sheepskins. Kell helped Hornwollen to one of them. Nicholas sat down in the other, and Kell disappeared up the steps.

Nicholas stared around him. There were paintings on the walls, done in a silvery-white paint. Some of them were of birds flying. One was of a walrus, and one was of a great bear.

Nicholas sat quite still, staring at the paintings. When at last he looked at Hornwollen, he saw that Hornwollen was watching him, smiling.

"I was just as amazed as you are, when the People of the Snow first brought me here," Hornwollen said. "I was lost in the snow, with the winter coming on. I was almost dead, when they found me. They carried me here, and I stayed with them until the spring. Then they gave me the house I live in now. They're a wonderful people.

"You've nothing to be afraid of. They'll help us. You can be sure of that."

"Who is the Ecrun?" asked Nicholas.

"That's the name they give to their ruler," said Hornwollen.

Kell came back down the steps, with two other men.

"The Ecrun will see you," he said. "We're to carry you up. The boy is to come, too."

They had brought a kind of seat, with

straps, for Hornwollen. One of them, a big man, strapped the seat to his back, and the other two lifted Hornwollen into it.

Then the big man turned, and went back up the steps, carrying Hornwollen. Nicholas followed him.

The rock staircase led up into another big room. It was lighted by silver lanterns. Banners hung from the rock walls, and there was a big table, made of some kind of silvery metal, standing in it.

They went higher and higher, along passages and through rooms. Everywhere was lit by the silver lanterns, but as they got higher, Nicholas saw that great windows had been cut in the rock, too. Captain Harken had been right. The caves they could see from below had been partly shaped and carved by men.

There were many beautiful things in the rooms, made from the silvery metal. There were tables, and lanterns, and chairs. More banners hung from the walls. Some of these had red and blue backgrounds, with pictures worked on them in silver thread.

But Nicholas was less interested in the things than the people. There were snow people everywhere. They stopped what they were doing, and gazed at Hornwollen and Nicholas as they went by.

There were women and children, as well as men. Some of them were working with metal, hammering and shaping it. Some of them were weaving the white, silvery cloth, of which all their clothes seemed to be made.

Some of them were cooking: they went through one room, where there was a table where all kinds of foods were being prepared. The food was being cooked over little metal stoves, which shone like silver.

At last they came to a silver curtain, across a passage near the top of the rock castle. Kell helped Hornwollen to get down from the chair. He pulled the curtain aside, and they went into the room.

It was a beautiful room with big windows looking out over the ice-covered sea. There was a low table in the middle of it. Chairs were drawn up around the table, and eleven of the snow people were sitting in them. Both the men and the women were dressed like Kell, but they had long cloaks, fastened to their shoulders by silver brooches. They wore silver chains around their waists.

One of them wore a chain around his neck, too. It had a circle of silver on the end of it. He looked up, as Hornwollen and the others came in. It was the Ecrun, the leader of the People of the Snow.

"You have come here with a stranger, Hornwollen?" he questioned. His eyes were stern, and he didn't smile.

"Yes," said Hornwollen. "I know you don't want strangers to discover you, here in the north. But I had to bring this boy.

"His ship went south, when the ice came

down from the north. He was lost in the fog, and they had to leave him behind.

"He would have died, without anyone to help him. You saved me, when I was lost. I was sure that you would save him, too.

"And he saved my life. I fell and twisted my foot in the berry-fields. A bear came. The boy drove the bear away, by blowing that horn, which hangs around his neck."

The Ecrun's face changed. He looked much more friendly.

"Come and sit down," he said.

Hornwollen and Nicholas crossed the room, and sat down at the table with the others. Nicholas looked at their faces. They were not unfriendly, but they looked watchful.

"You came in the ship we have seen?" the Ecrun asked Nicholas. "The ship with a bird carved under its bowsprit?"

"*The Snow Goose*," said Nicholas. "Yes. I came in *The Snow Goose*."

"Where did you come from?"

Nicholas told them about Captain Harken and the buccaneers. He told them about Ramir, and why they had come north.

"So you have come for the scarlet snow-berries," said the Ecrun. "Well, I can understand that."

He was silent for a moment, looking at Nicholas.

"Do the buccaneers hunt whales?" he asked suddenly.

Nicholas shook his head. "No," he said. "They catch fish for food. They don't hunt whales. The whales are our friends."

"Do the buccaneers want to stay up here in the north?" asked the Ecrun.

"How do you mean? Stay here?" asked Nicholas. "I don't understand. They couldn't *stay* here, in all the ice and cold."

"We have had men from the south here before," said the Ecrun. "They hunted whales. They built stone houses, over on the East Land, near the berry-fields, where you met Hornwollen. They claimed the berry-fields as their own. They hunted and killed our white hares. They didn't just take the scarlet berries. They killed everything, and they took everything."

He paused for a moment, and his face hardened.

"We drove them away with the help of the Ice King," he said.

Nicholas swallowed. "The buccaneers don't want to stay here," he said. "I'm sure they don't. All they want are some scarlet berries, to take back to Ramir. People are dying in Ramir, and only the berries can save them.

"We saw the white hares, but nobody touched them. And they'll trade with you for the berries. I know they will."

The Ecrun looked at Nicholas for such a long time, without saying anything, that Nicholas felt his face growing red.

"Did you meet any other ship, as you came north?" the Ecrun asked suddenly, leaning forward in his chair.

"We met the Arcons," said Nicholas.

"Are they friends of yours?"

"We made friends with them," said Nicholas.

He saw the Ecrun's face harden again.

"Shouldn't we be friends with them?" he asked.

"They have settled on our land," said the Ecrun. "We used to take our sheep there in the summer, before the Arcons came."

"They don't know that it's your land," said Nicholas.

"They will learn before long," said the Ecrun.

He sat back in his chair and thought for a moment.

"At least you have told us the truth," he said. "We knew that you had met the Arcons."

"I'm sure you can trust the boy," said Hornwollen quietly. "And *The Snow Goose* comes from Ramir. The men from the south, the ones who killed the whales and stole the berries — they came from Alunka, not from Ramir."

The Ecrun nodded. "That is true, Hornwollen," he said. "You came from Ramir, too. We have always found that we could trust you."

There was silence.

"Leave us for a few minutes," the Ecrun said at last. "We must talk about this."

Hornwollen and Nicholas got up. Kell took them to a little room, not far away, and left them there. There were two chairs in the room. Each chair was covered with the strange, silvery white cloth.

"Where does the cloth come from?" asked Nicholas, as they sat down.

"They spin it from a metal they find underground," said Hornwollen. "It keeps out the cold. They make their clothes from it, too. They dig it out, when they dig out their rock castles.

"They are a strange people, Nicholas. Some people say that they can work all kinds of magic. I'm not sure. It may be that they know more than the rest of us. They have discovered many kinds of different metals in the rocks. They have found many strange plants, too, growing on the slopes where the snow melts in the summer. They use those for food, and for medicines. And they catch fish.

"They are indeed a strange people. If they accept you as a friend, they will do everything they can for you. But if they think you are an enemy — well, let's hope they know you're a friend."

Kell came into the room.

"Come," he said.

They went back to the big room with him. The Ecrun beckoned them to sit down at the table.

"We have decided to help you, Nicholas," he said quietly. "But first, I want you to promise me something. Hornwollen tells me that we can trust you. Very well. We will. We want you to promise that you will never tell anyone about the rock castles, or the fact that we live in them."

"I promise," said Nicholas.

"You will not tell *anyone*? Not even Captain Harken and the buccaneers?"

"I won't tell anyone at all," said Nicholas. "I promise."

The Ecrun nodded, as if he was satisfied.

"Then we can help you," he said. "While we were talking, the seabirds brought us news.

"A boat is trying to make its way north through the ice. It has come from *The Snow Goose.* The ship is waiting for the boat, to the south of the ice-floes. The buccaneers must be coming back to find you."

"They'll be coming back to look for snowberries," said Nicholas. "If they found any before the fog came, they would be sure to come back."

"Perhaps," said the Ecrun. "But, whatever they have come for, they will soon be in great danger. The weather is changing. There is a storm coming. In this country, the weather can change in an hour. Already, the wind is rising.

"The storm will bring a great mass of ice with it, down from the north. *The Snow Goose* will have to sail south — or be crushed in the ice. And the men in the small boat will never survive, if we don't help them.

"We are going out, to try to reach them."

"Can I go with you?" asked Nicholas.

The Ecrun looked at him.

"It will be very dangerous, even for us," he said.

"I must go," said Nicholas. "They're my friends. I've been in danger before."

"Very well," said the Ecrun. "You can come with us. Indeed, it will be the easiest way to take you back to your friends.

"Get him some proper clothes, Kell, and bring him down to the outer door, as quickly as you can. We shall leave from there."

Chapter 9
The loss of the jolly boat

A few minutes later, Nicholas was back in the room at the foot of the stairs. He was dressed in a white tunic and trousers, like the People of the Snow, and he had on a thick, white parka (Nicholas called it an anorak) over his tunic. It had a hood, fringed with tiny strips of metal. He pulled it over his head, and fastened it under his chin. He was wearing long, soft boots, too, like Hornwollen's, and white mittens over the gloves on his hands. He felt very warm, and he looked just like one of the snow people.

The others were already there. The Ecrun himself seemed to be in charge.

"Is the Ecrun going?" Nicholas whispered to Hornwollen.

"Of course," said Hornwollen. "It will be very dangerous. The Ecrun is the leader of his people. He's the wisest man among them. Of course he'll go."

"I bet Captain Harken's in that boat," Nicholas whispered. "He'd go, too, if there was real danger."

Hornwollen smiled.

"I must say goodbye to you, Nicholas," he said. "My foot hurts too much, to let me come with you, and I must go back to Kuluk. The snow people will help you now."

"What about the scarlet berries?" asked Nicholas.

"I think they will give you those, too. But you must leave that to them," said Hornwollen quietly. "Thank you for all your help, boy. Tell them in Ramir that I am living safely in the north."

"I will," said Nicholas.

The Ecrun looked around, and saw that everyone was there. There were twenty snow people, including the Ecrun. The Ecrun was wearing the same clothes as the others, but there was a round, silver disc on his hood. He signalled with his hand to one of the snow people. The door in the rock opened. Nicholas said a last 'goodbye' to Hornwollen, and they went outside.

He was surprised to see how quickly everything had changed. The wind was rising, and dark clouds were blowing up. The ice was heaving on the sea. It was already moving southwards, blown by the wind. Great masses of ice were moving down from the north.

There were ten boats drawn up beside the rock. They were like Hornwollen's boat, but a little bigger. Six of them were laden with stores, packed in the white, silvery cloth. The other four boats were empty.

Two of the snow people got into each boat, and picked up the paddles. The Ecrun beckoned to Nicholas to join him. Nicholas clambered into the middle of the boat, between the Ecrun, who was in the stern, and another one of the snow people, who was in the bows.

The Ecrun lifted his paddle as a signal, and they set off, across the ice-filled sea.

* * *

Farther south, the buccaneers in the jolly boat were making their way slowly north through the ice-floes. They were having to struggle every bit of the way, against the wind and against the current. The wind was bitterly cold, and blowing hard from the north. The men were very tired.

As far as they could see from the boat, the sea in every direction was covered with floating ice.

"The weather has changed, and it's getting worse," said Captain Harken. "We'll pull in by that ice-floe over there, and see if we can get some shelter."

They pulled in close to a great mass of ice, and threw an anchor across from the stern and another from the bows of the boat.

"There's a storm coming," said Peran, looking at the sky.

The wind was rising, and great dark clouds were sweeping up from the north. The great rafts of ice tossed on the swell of the sea.

Then the snow came. At first, there were just a few flakes, but in a few minutes the air was thick with it. It was so cold, that the flakes were small and hard, more like hail than snow. It fell in great curtains all around them. It drove into the boat, and into their faces. On every side, they could see nothing but driving snow.

"We'll haul the boat out on the ice-floe, and get some shelter," said Captain Harken. "We'll have to wait till this is over. We'll camp, and have food, and get some sleep."

They pulled the boat in close to the ice, and climbed out on the floe. Captain Harken took a long pole from the boat, and walked about, driving it into the ice, testing the floe to make sure that it wouldn't give way under their feet.

When he thought it seemed safe, they hauled up the boat, and spread the sail over it, for shelter. It was a slow job. The wind kept catching the sail, and blowing it out of their frozen hands. But at last they managed to lash it down.

They crawled in under it, into the boat, and struggled into their sleeping bags, for warmth.

Cass handed round some food to each man, and they ate it, lying packed in the jolly boat like so many sardines in a tin.

Tiredness came over them, and they slept a little.

When they woke, the snow had stopped, but it was much colder. The outside of the sleeping bags had frozen, and the canvas sail covering the boat was like a board. With frozen fingers, they unlashed it enough to climb out on to the ice-floe.

They looked around them. Everywhere

they could see, the sea was a mass of heaving ice. The storm had brought it down from the north. The lanes of water had closed up, and the sea itself was beginning to freeze.

Cass looked at Captain Harken.

"Do we go on, Captain?" he asked.

Captain Harken looked out over the ice field. There was no chance of getting the boat back to open water. There was no open water to be seen. As far as he could see, the ice-floes were pushed together, looking like rolling hills of ice on the swell of the sea.

When he looked back, the way they had come, he could see that there was no chance of rowing there, either. The ice had closed up behind them. They were in the middle of a great field of ice, and it looked as if they had very little chance of getting out of it.

"We wait," he said quietly. "We had to do our best to get the berries, and we had to try to rescue Nicholas. But we can't get through this — not for a time, anyway. Perhaps winter has set in already. Perhaps this is just a storm, and the sea will open again, before the real winter comes. We don't know. But there's only one thing to do at the moment.

"We'll make ourselves as comfortable as we can where we are, and wait for the ice to break up a bit."

"Suppose it doesn't break up?" asked Downalong Joe.

"I think it will," said Captain Harken.

"Hadn't you noticed, Downalong? The wind is carrying the ice south. There's a current, too.

"We've been fighting our way north in the boat against the wind and the current. Now we'll wait here on the ice-floe, and let the wind and current carry us south again. I think it may break up, as it moves south."

"Suppose the whole ice field freezes solid for the winter?" asked Downalong.

"Then we'll make our way over it to the land," said Captain Harken. "There's land to the west. You can just see the mountains over there, white against the grey sky.

"But let's wait and see, Downalong. We'll take one thing at a time."

"It's a good thing we came in these clothes," said Peran. "We'd have been frozen, in the clothes we wore on *The Snow Goose*."

Captain Harken nodded. "We'll manage," he said. "We'll set up camp here, on the ice-floe. We'll haul the boat a bit farther on to the ice, and shake out the sleeping bags.

"Cass, see if you can get a fire going, and make us some hot food."

Everyone was soon working away, trying to make things more comfortable.

Cass took the flat stone, and the fuel they had brought with them.

He had a cow's horn, too. Little bits of dry cloth and sticks and grass had been pushed into the hollow inside of the horn. Cass took a bit of metal and a flint stone from a little bag, which was slung from his belt. He struck the metal with the flint. A spark flew up, and landed on the dry tinder in the cow's horn.

Cass lifted the horn quickly to his mouth, and blew gently on the spark. A little flame flared up among the tinder.

Cass dropped the burning tinder on the flat stone, and piled up some sticks around it. He soon had a fire going.

He set a pot full of stew on the fire, and heated it.

The hot food warmed everyone, and cheered them up, too. They shook the ice off their sleeping bags, and cleared it out of the boat. They managed to unlash the sail, and stow it in the boat again.

Captain Harken worked with them, encouraging them all the time.

Then some of the men lay down in the boat, and slept, while the others built a wall of ice, to shelter them from the wind.

They explored the ice-floe, on which they found themselves. It was like a very big, wide, rough field, with hummocks of ice everywhere.

In one place, they found some fish, which had been flung up on to the ice in the storm, and frozen there. They collected the fish for supper.

The wind dropped. It was growing colder

all the time, but the cold was easier to bear, without the wind.

After a time, the men changed places, and Captain Harken and the others slept.

They were all awake, and eating a hot meal together, when they saw a bird high up above them. The bird swung down and circled around them, as if it was looking at them. Then it flew up high again, and headed north.

"If only we were near the Island of Solomon Dee, I'd say that was one of his friends!" exclaimed Downalong. "And how I wish it was!"

"I'm surprised there are any birds up here, with winter coming on," said Captain Harken. "You'd think they would all have flown south."

He got up.

"The wind's getting up again," he said. "But it's changing. It's swinging around to the south. The ice came in so quickly, that it could blow out quickly, too."

* * *

Three hours later, the wind was blowing a gale. The ice-floes were rolling on the sea. Cracks were appearing everywhere about them. The ice heaved and groaned like a living thing.

A great crack appeared in the ice on the far side of the boat.

"Get across to the boat!" cried Captain

Harken. "The ice is breaking up again. Take everything with you. Quickly."

They picked up the fire stone and what was left of the food, and struggled across the ice to the boat.

As they did so, the crack widened, and a lane of water appeared. They heard the ice beginning to break up farther away from them.

"Do we push her into the sea, Captain?" cried Peran, as they reached the boat.

"Not yet," cried Captain Harken. "It's too dangerous."

Even as he spoke, the ice on each side of the crack crashed together again, and a wave of foaming water rushed up over the ice.

The ice under their feet cracked wide open. Cass stumbled, lost his footing, and fell into the water.

Before he could sink, Captain Harken seized him by the shoulders, and heaved him up, out on the ice again. He was only just in time, before the crack closed like a vice.

"Push the boat farther on to the ice! Quickly!" shouted Captain Harken. "We've got to wait till there's open water, or the boat will be crushed between the floes."

They dumped the things in the boat, and heaved and pushed in the only direction which still seemed safe. At least everyone was warm. Even Cass, who was half soaked with water, managed to push with the rest, and warm himself a little.

When they thought the boat was safe, they climbed into her, and waited. Cass dried himself as well as he could, while Peran cooked some hot food.

The hours passed slowly. The wind went on blowing. It grew stronger and stronger. Slowly, all around them, the ice field began to break up. Wider and wider lanes of water appeared.

Suddenly, a great crack widened in the ice under the boat. The ice broke apart, and the boat fell through into the water. Then, before they could do anything at all, the two sides of the crack crashed together, catching the boat between them.

"On to the ice-floe!" cried Captain Harken. "Jump for it!"

He bent down, seized the sack of food, and flung it on to the ice. Peran jumped with the pot of stew, and landed safely. The ice held the boat fast for a few minutes, and in that time, Captain Harken and Downalong flung the sleeping bags and the other sacks from the boat out on to the ice.

They clambered down after them, dragging the sail with them. The other buccaneers, who were now on the ice, stumbled forward to give them a hand. They cut the ropes and pulled the sail clear.

The wooden sides of the boat cracked and broke as if they were no stronger than eggshells. The ice groaned under their feet, and

the crack began to open again. Water swelled up into the boat.

"Back!" cried Captain Harken. "Back for your lives!"

The buccaneers staggered back, laden with gear from the boat.

The crack widened. The boat filled with water. It tilted forwards, and dived down below the ice.

The buccaneers stood for a few moments as if they had been frozen into statues. It seemed to each one of them, that they would soon follow the boat into the sea.

Captain Harken was the first man to pull himself together.

"We'll move back still farther," he said. "Get right into the middle of this patch of ice. Bring the things with you. This way."

The buccaneers stumbled across the ice after him. He led the way to some great chunks of ice, right in the centre.

"How long do you think it will be, before this breaks up, Captain?" asked Downalong, as he dumped the sail down on the ice.

"It's hard to tell, Downalong," said Captain Harken. "Let's hope the sea freezes first. But it's no good thinking ahead. We've got to do the best we can now.

"Let's turn that sail into a shelter."

They found a place where they could spread the sail over some broken chunks of ice, to make a kind of tent for themselves. They pulled the sleeping bags, and whatever food they had left, into the shelter. They huddled together for warmth.

Captain Harken spoke as cheerfully as he could, but they all knew that, with the boat gone, they hadn't much chance of seeing *The Snow Goose* again.

Chapter 10
A horn blows

On the same ice field, farther north, Nicholas lay propped up on one arm, on a warm sleeping bag, inside a big white tent. The tent was shaped like an upturned bowl. It was made of the strange, silvery white cloth the ice people used, and it was very comfortable.

There was a little stove in the middle of the tent, and the glowing metal inside it warmed the air. One of the snow people was busy cooking over the stove, and the others were sitting around on their sleeping bags, talking cheerfully.

It was some hours since they had climbed out of their boats on to the ice. The snow people had pulled the boats up, out of the water. As Nicholas watched, they had pulled out little rolls of metal which had opened up, like telescopes, to make the poles for the big round tent.

In no time at all, it seemed to Nicholas, they had stretched the silver cloth over the poles, and laid more cloth down as a carpet on the ice. In a few minutes, they were all resting safely inside the tent. The stove was pouring out heat, and the food was cooking. Then they had all slept. Now they were awake again, and getting ready to eat, before they moved on.

"We'll have to travel over the ice," said

the Ecrun, as they sat there, eating. "We'll take to the water where we can. But the ice is closing up, and we'll have to use boats as sledges, now."

Nicholas discovered what that meant when they went outside. The ice had closed up, and stretched as far as he could see, in every direction.

The snow people lifted their boats, and fixed light runners to them. The runners were made of the same light metal as the boats.

Then they packed everything into the boats, and fastened silver ropes to the bows. Each man put on snow-shoes, for crossing the ice, and they set out, hauling on the ropes, and pulling the boats behind them.

They had given Nicholas snow-shoes, too. Nicholas found that he was very clumsy with them to begin with, but as they went on, he got more used to them.

The Ecrun went first, choosing the path across the snow that had fallen on the ice. The others followed in his tracks. The sun was low in the sky, but it never dropped below the horizon, and they could see the ice stretching out ahead of them.

They travelled on, hour after hour. From time to time, they came across a wide lane of water, and the sledges became boats again. But it was never long before they had to be hauled out once more on the ice. It was hard work, and Nicholas became very tired.

After a while, they turned south-west, and

Nicholas saw snow-covered mountains far ahead of them, above a white bank of fog.

Twice, one of the seabirds swung down out of the sky, and perched by the Ecrun, calling and clicking its beak, in a way which reminded Nicholas of Solomon's sea-fishers. The second time, the Ecrun turned and spoke to Nicholas, as the bird flew off.

"Your friends are not far ahead of us now," he said. "But their boat has been crushed in the ice. They are out on one of the ice-floes. I hope we shall reach them before long. The fog will be down again soon."

Nicholas gazed at him anxiously. He had already seen that they were moving towards the fog bank — or the fog was moving towards them. The Ecrun looked at his white face.

"We are travelling as fast as we can, Nicholas," he said. "But if the fog comes down, we shall have to camp for a time. The birds won't be able to guide us, and we might go past them in the fog."

The boats, which were also sledges, sped on even faster over the ice.

Half an hour later, the fog rolled over them. It was as if a white blanket had suddenly fallen all about them.

The Ecrun stopped, and the other boat-sledges came up to him.

"We will camp here," he said. "We are on a solid pillar of ice. It stretches down into the sea below us. They can't be far ahead now, but we must wait for the fog to lift, or we shall miss them."

"The ice field is beginning to break up again," said one of the snow people quietly.

Nicholas had noticed that the lanes of water were getting wider, but now everything was hidden by fog.

He suddenly remembered that he still had his horn around his neck. He tore his parka open, and pulled it out.

"Couldn't we go on?" he said. "I could blow the horn. They'd hear it. If they're not far ahead, we might find them."

The Ecrun looked at him. "Can they reply, if they hear you?" he asked.

"Captain Harken will have his horn with him," said Nicholas. "I'm sure he will."

The Ecrun nodded.

"We'll go a little farther, then," he said. "From what the birds say, they can't be far. Sound your horn, Nicholas. We'll go on for a while, and see if we can find them."

* * *

The fog lay thick over the whole ice field.

The raft of ice, where the buccaneers were huddling in their tent, was beginning to break up. Another great crack had appeared, and split off a big corner of it. They had found themselves so close to the water, that they had shifted camp. Before long, they had to move again.

"We'll have to try and get across to another ice-raft," said Captain Harken.

The ice shook under their feet, as the sea rolled under it, and another chunk of ice crashed into it, breaking still more off the edge.

"The whole ice field's breaking up," said Downalong. "Where are we going to jump to? You can't see anything, in this fog."

"Look out!" cried Peran.

A crack widened under their feet. They leapt aside, and the ice parted, leaving Cass and Peran on one side, and Captain Harken and the other buccaneers on the other. Their raft of ice had split right down the middle.

"This way!" shouted Cass.

Cass and Peran were on the smaller piece. They ran across to an icy hummock on the edge of the crack. Cass jumped, and Peran followed.

As they landed on the far side, the crack widened still farther, and the two parts of ice drifted apart.

"We nearly lost you that time, Cass!" said Downalong Joe.

"We're all lost!" cried Alwar. "We're all lost! Look! Look what we've left behind!"

The buccaneers stared at the patch of ice which was floating away from them. Their bundles of food, and the sleeping bags, were drifting away on it.

Downalong Joe started to pull off his clothes.

"I'll swim for it!" he cried.

"Don't be a fool, Downalong!" cried Captain Harken. "You won't live for five minutes in that water. You'll freeze to death before you can reach the ice."

"We'll all freeze to death, without food and shelter!" said Alwar.

Far off in the fog, a horn sounded.

The buccaneers stood still, staring at one another.

The sound came again.

Captain Harken pushed his hand in under his clothes, and pulled out his own horn.

As he lifted it to his lips, Alwar caught his arm.

"Don't blow, Captain!" he cried. "Don't answer! Who would call to us, across the ice? It'll be the People of the Snow! They're ghosts! They'll capture us. That's what the Arcons said!"

Captain Harken threw off his arm.

"Ghosts or not, they're our only chance, Alwar," he said.

He lifted the horn to his lips again, and blew.

At once, the far off horn sounded again. It was nearer this time. And again Captain Harken answered it.

"That's not a ghost!" he cried. "That's one of the horns of the Strange Land. Don't you know the sound? They've found us! They've found us in time!"

Boats came out of the mist. The men at

their paddles were dressed in the silvery white cloth, that looked like snow.

"They're ghosts!" cried Alwar, starting back in fear. "They're ghosts — or snow people!"

"Captain Harken!" shouted Nicholas. "It's me! Nicholas! We've come to rescue you."

Captain Harken gripped Alwar's arm, and held him still.

"Nicholas!" he cried. "Nicholas!"

"The boy's dead! It's his ghost!" cried Alwar, struggling to get away.

"Don't be afraid!" cried the Ecrun, who was paddling the leading boat. "We are the People of the Snow, but you needn't be afraid. We've come to help you."

The boat ran alongside the raft of ice. Nicholas climbed quickly out, and stumbled across the ice to the buccaneers.

"I'm not dead!" he cried. "I'm as alive as you are! The snow people are our friends. They're people, like us — it's only their clothes that make them look like the snow."

"I can see that," said Captain Harken. "And I can't tell you how glad we are to see you, Nicholas — and to see the snow people. Alwar was startled just now."

He dropped Alwar's arm, and stepped forward to greet the Ecrun.

Alwar stood still. He was still shaking, and he looked very white.

Peran threw an arm around his shoulder.

"If young Nick is a friend of the snow people, so am I, and so are you!" he said cheerfully. "I'm willing to be friends with anyone who'll take me off this raft of ice before it breaks up! They've saved us, Alwar. We'd have been ghosts ourselves, before very long. There's nothing to be afraid of. It's only young Nick and his friends!"

The snow people had arrived only just in time. The buccaneers had scarcely scrambled into their rescuers' boats, when the ice they had been standing on split from end to end.

* * *

When the buccaneers reached the ice-floe, they found that some of the snow people had set up two big bowl-shaped tents, and hot food was ready inside them.

The buccaneers sat down thankfully in the warmth of one of the tents, and pulled off their heavy parkas.

One of the snow people brought them bowls of hot stew, and goblets full of a kind of wine.

The wine, too, was hot. It had been poured over nuts and dried berries, and it tasted very good. The hot drink seemed to run through their veins like fire, warming them from the tops of their heads right down to their toes.

"I can scarcely believe we're here," said Cass, as he drained his goblet. "Are you sure we haven't fallen asleep on the ice? I feel as if I'm in a dream."

"If this is a dream, I don't want to wake up!" said Peran cheerfully. He was sitting next to Alwar. The colour had come back to Alwar's face. He looked around him in amazement, as he drank his hot wine.

"It's no dream," said Captain Harken, as one of the snow people ladled some more hot stew into his bowl. "We're awake, and we're safe, and I think we've found friends."

The Ecrun came into the tent, and Captain Harken struggled to his feet.

"We can never thank you enough," he said. "We owe you our lives."

"Don't think of it," said the Ecrun. "Up here in the north, one or other of us needs help every day. We all owe our lives to each other.

"Your young Nicholas saved Hornwollen from a bear. Did you know that?"

"I didn't know it, but I'm not surprised," said Captain Harken. "Did you say 'Hornwollen'? Is he here?"

"He is in his home in the north," said the Ecrun. "He would have come, but he had hurt his foot."

"Hornwollen is the greatest traveller who has ever gone out from Ramir," said Captain Harken. "I'm glad to know that he is with you. We thought he must be dead.

"I'm glad Nicholas was there to help him, too. And I'm very thankful that you were there, to help us."

"We saved you from the ice today," said the Ecrun. "Perhaps it will be your turn to save us tomorrow."

"If there is anything we can ever do for you, you have only to ask," said Captain Harken.

"I have only one thing to ask," said the Ecrun. "And that is, that you leave us in peace, here in the north. This is our land — the Land of the Snow. We have learned to live in this land. It is a hard land, a cold land — and a very beautiful land. Leave us to live here in peace."

"But of course we will," said Captain Harken. "We came here only for one thing: we were looking for the scarlet berries of the snow."

The Ecrun nodded. "That is what the boy said," he answered. "We have ten sacks of the dried berries ready for you, packed in our boats."

"Ten sacks of the scarlet berries of the snow?" cried Captain Harken. "That would cure all the illness in Ramir!"

"They are ready for you to take to Ramir," said the Ecrun. "They are a gift to you, from the People of the Snow. And for you yourself, there is one of our metal stoves. Bring it with you, if ever you travel again in the north. It will keep you warm, if you have to camp on the ice. It could save your life."

"I will take your gifts very gladly," said Captain Harken. "We owe you even more thanks for the berries than we owe you for our lives. And I will keep the stove, and remember what you have said."

"All we ask is that we shall be left in peace," said the Ecrun.

"We will leave you in peace," said Captain Harken. "We shall go south as soon as we can. We must get the berries to Ramir as soon as possible. But I'm afraid *The Snow Goose* may have sailed already. They will have sailed when the ice came down from the north. They'll think that we are dead. We should have been dead, but for you."

"*The Snow Goose* was still sailing north when the birds last saw her," said the Ecrun. "I can see that the men of Ramir don't easily leave their friends behind. You may have come back for the berries, but you also came back for the boy?"

Captain Harken nodded. "Of course I did," he said.

"Then I think the men on *The Snow Goose* are coming back for you," said the Ecrun. "You must sleep first, and then we will travel south. I shall be surprised if we do not find your friends still looking for you."

Chapter 11
The journey home

The storm from the north had driven the ice south.

As the storm raged, Barnabas Brandy and Tom Gold watched great fields of ice sweep down past *The Snow Goose,* until there was no longer enough open water to sail the ship.

They found themselves in a channel, with ice to the north of them, and on both sides.

"We'll have to turn south for a bit, Barnabas," said Tom Gold. "There's a real storm coming."

They were standing on the poop deck, watching the sea.

"How can we do that, when Captain Harken and the others are out there in the boat?" Barnabas almost shouted at Tom Gold. He knew that Tom was right, but he couldn't bear to give orders which would take *The Snow Goose* farther away from Captain Harken. "They may be trying to make their way back to the ship at this very moment!"

"It won't help them, if the ship has been smashed up by the ice, Barnabas," said Tom quietly. "We've got to move south while we can. If the wind shifts, the ice fields will break up, and we can sail north again — if we've got a ship to sail in. If the ship has been sunk by the ice, there will be nothing we can do to save them."

Barnabas stared at him for a moment.

Then he swung on his heel, and shouted some orders to the men.

He turned back to Tom Gold.

"You're right, Tom," he said. "I know you are. But I can't forget that I left Nick behind. And now we've got to leave Captain Harken and the others."

"You mustn't let that stop you sailing the ship, Barnabas," said Tom Gold. "Put it behind you. If you think of nothing but that, you'll wreck *The Snow Goose.* And what good will that do?

"Captain Harken gave you your orders. If the ice came down, we were to leave, and sail south. The thing that matters most, is to save *The Snow Goose.*"

The Snow Goose had been carrying two boats. Captain Harken had taken the jolly boat. Now the long boat was lowered into the water. Eight men climbed down into her, and took *The Snow Goose* in tow.

They were being driven south by the wind and current. The main job of the rowers in the long boat was to keep *The Snow Goose* in the middle of the channel of open water. The wind drove *The Snow Goose* south, but the wind came in gusts. It could change at any moment, and Barnabas knew that he mustn't let the ship crash into the ice on either side of them.

A storm of snow swept across them, blotting out everything that was more than twenty metres away from the ship.

When the snow cleared, they saw more channels of open water ahead of them to the west. Icebergs were moving down with the ice field, swept along by the wind and the sea.

The men in the long boat did their best, but every now and again, the side of the ship cannoned against a piece of floating ice. When that happened, they felt the whole ship shudder under them.

Hour after hour went by. Barnabas changed the rowers in the long boat from time to time. Towing the ship was exhausting work.

After a long time, they reached a wider patch of open water. Barnabas called in the long boat, and got enough sail on the ship to steer her. The wind was still blowing from the north.

The Snow Goose turned south-west, and sailed until she came to the edge of another great ice field. Then she went about, and sailed south-east, until she met the ice in that direction. She couldn't turn north, and sail into the wind. In any case, Barnabas knew that the ice was sweeping down behind them.

When at last the wind dropped, they came across an iceberg which was large and fairly flat. They could see a great shelf of ice under the water, stretching out in front of it, but the ice cliffs on one side went down straight into the sea.

Barnabas anchored *The Snow Goose* to the side of the iceberg. They still travelled south with it, but they travelled much more slowly. The current still carried them south, but there was so much ice in the sea below the berg that the wind didn't make much difference to its speed.

The wind changed at last, and began to swing round to the south. But for a long time, *The Snow Goose* could not sail for the north again. There was too much ice in the sea. Great fields of ice had come down in the wind and current.

Barnabas was like a cat on hot bricks. He couldn't rest. Tom Gold did his best to calm him. But every buccaneer on *The Snow Goose* knew that Captain Harken and the others must be in great danger.

As soon as there was any chance of making their way through the ice fields, *The Snow Goose* took in her anchors, and turned north.

* * *

Two days later, Barnabas Brandy was on the deck of *The Snow Goose.* He was looking out over the sea.

The sky was blue overhead, and icebergs floated by on the dark water. But the ice field had broken up, and *The Snow Goose* was still sailing north.

Tom Gold had gone up into the barrel at the cross-trees himself. He had Captain Harken's telescope with him. Every now and then he put it to his eye, and swept the sea with it.

Suddenly, he stiffened.

"Barnabas!" he shouted. "Barnabas! I think — I think I can see them!"

"What?" cried Barnabas. "Can you see the boat?"

"Not the jolly boat," cried Tom Gold. "There are ten bits of ice out there, moving this way. At least, they look as white as the ice. But each bit is shaped like a boat, and I think it's the captain and the others sitting in them. Yes — they're dressed in skins, just like the captain. But — I can't believe it!"

"What is it?" cried Barnabas.

"The boats are being paddled by snowmen!" shouted Tom Gold.

Barnabas Brandy stared at the sea ahead. He could just make out some white shapes, moving on the water, a long way away.

"Bring that spy-glass down here, Tom!" he cried. "We can see them from the deck now."

Tom Gold climbed quickly down the rigging, and handed him the telescope. Barnabas put it to his eye.

"It's the captain, all right," he said. "The others are there, too. All six of them. But the men paddling the boats...!"

"They're the People of the Snow," said Tom Gold. "They must be."

"You're right," said Barnabas, handing him back the telescope. "So there really are

People of the Snow! I don't care whether they can work magic, as the Arcons say, or not. If they're bringing the captain safely back, they're welcome, whoever they are!"

By the time the boats were within hailing distance of the ship, all the buccaneers were on deck, staring over the side.

"Hallo there, Barnabas!" shouted Captain Harken. "Lower the rope ladders, and tell the cook to prepare a feast. We're safely home, and we've brought friends with us. Nicholas, too."

"Nicholas?" cried Barnabas Brandy and Tom Gold together.

Nicholas waved.

"The boy's turned into a snowman!" said Barnabas.

"It's his clothes," said Tom Gold. "If that's Nicholas in all that white stuff, then the others are men, too."

He stared at them for a moment longer, and then turned to the buccaneers.

"Lower the rope ladders!" he cried. "What are you waiting for? Can't you see that the captain's back, and he's brought friends with him?"

* * *

Four hours later, as the sun rose slowly in the sky, *The Snow Goose* was sailing south. Captain Harken was on deck with Barnabas Brandy.

The People of the Snow had gone. The boats of the snow people had set off for home laden with gifts: with barrels of flour and wine, and jars of honey, and golden brooches and necklaces from Ramir.

The ten sacks of dried scarlet berries were safely in the hold of *The Snow Goose.*

As the snow people had left the ship, the Ecrun had turned back to Captain Harken.

"If you need more berries in the years to come, come back," he had said. "The birds will see you coming, and bring us the news, and we will come and meet you.

"I trust you, Captain Harken. We will help you if we can."

"We will come," said Captain Harken. "We will come when we need the berries. And you can trust us to go back to Ramir again, and leave you in peace. You have my word for that."

* * *

"Well, they've gone, Francis," said Barnabas Brandy, as the wind caught the sails, and *The Snow Goose* glided south over a calm sea. "The scarlet berries are safely in the hold, and we're on our way back to Ramir. I'm as glad to have the boy safely back with us, as I am to have the berries."

Captain Harken smiled. "The Ecrun said that Nicholas saved Hornwollen from a bear," he said.

''Saved Hornwollen from a bear!'' cried Barnabas Brandy. ''Hornwollen! Where is he? And what happened? When did they meet a bear?''

''Ask Nicholas to tell you the story himself,'' said Captain Harken. ''Look. He's over there, by the bows.''

But as they walked across the deck to Nicholas, the light on the sea in front of the ship seemed suddenly to grow brighter. A great ring of silver spun off the water into the air, as though it had been thrown by a giant's hand.

The ring fell around Nicholas, and blazed up, like silver fire. Then died away.

Captain Harken and Barnabas Brandy stood staring at the empty deck. Nicholas had gone back to his own world.